THE HELL PLANET

THE HELL PLANET

E. C. TUBB

WILDSIDE PRESS

CHAPTER I

They stood on a vast, rolling plain of greyish dust, a barren desert dropping swiftly towards the near horizon of the tiny world. Three of them, three men, each dressed in heavy spacesuits, their helmets, and armour polished to a mirror finish so that they flashed and scintillated as they moved, looking like creatures clothed in light, resplendent with reflected brilliance.

Above their heads an enormous sun, fully nine times as large as seen from Earth, shone blue against an airless sky of midnight black. Flames shot from it, spinning into space, over a quarter of a million miles tall and seeming to move with majestic slowness and yet, as they rose they travelled at more than a hundred thousand miles a second. The sun hung motionless in the heavens, and near it, for all its searing brilliance, stars were visible, for there was no scattering or shielding air to spread its light into hazing brightness. Strange were those stars nearest to the sun, seeming to writhe and move, to be distorted and warped from normal space, for even light has mass, and the tremendous gravitational field of the sun bent the light passing through it.

On the plain, shimmering as the armoured men shimmered, as all things had to shimmer on the day side of Mercury, rested a vehicle. It was low and round like an egg cut down its long axis, and wide treads showed beneath the polished metal of the hull. It was tilted a little, dropped at one side, and sheared metal showed bright where no sheared metal should be.

Dennison stared at it, squinting even through the laminated glare-shields of his faceplate, then nudged the switch of the inter-suit radio with his chin.

"Any luck, Anders?"

"No." A man straightened from where he crouched beside the crippled vehicle and his voice echoed thinly from the receiver, distorted even at this distance with blurring static. "The tread's gone, sheared clean from the driving wheels, and a couple of links are broken."

"Can we repair it?" The third man spoke, and Dennison frowned at the thin edge of hysteria in his voice.

"I don't know. Can we, Anders?"

"No."

"We must!" This time there was no mistaking the hysteria in the thin tones. "We've got to!"

"We'll do what we can, Hendris," snapped Dennison sharply. "Maybe you'd better get back in the shell and take a rest."

"Yes." There was pitiful eagerness in the thin voice. "Thank you. I feel as though I'm stifling in this suit."

"Maybe we'd all better get inside," suggested Anders. "Nothing we can do out here except talk, and we may as well do that in comfort."

"Right." Dennison nodded, a sheer habit reflex, forgetting the others couldn't possibly see his gesture. "Hendris will go first, then you, Anders, and I'll come last Hurry it up now and don't lose more air than you can help."

Patiently he waited as first the geologist, then the engineer, entered the small airlock of the vehicle, and while waiting glared irritably at several columns of writhing dust which suddenly rose all around him. Even as he stared the twisting columns, some as tall as a man, others three times as high, collapsed, falling back to the plain from which they sprang. Then they rose again, thicker and stronger than before, swirling and taking on a vague suggestion of shape.

For a moment it seemed as if a face peered at him, an idiotic visage, slack mouthed and with hollow eyes, then it was gone, changing to battlemented spires and soaring arches. Other columns shifted into fantastic suggestions of weird beasts, enigmatic machines, oddly fashioned rocks, and once, for a brief moment, something that could have been a miniature spaceship.

All around him they swirled in ever-changing clouds of spinning dust, and within his helmet tiny instruments registered the presence of surging, external energies. As usual Dennison was half-fascinated, half-annoyed at the dust columns, fascinated because of their constantly changing pattern, and annoyed because even after twenty years sojourn on Mercury men still didn't know just what they were.

Electrical, of course, the instruments showed that. A surge of electro-magnetic currents, spinning at random over the planet, born from the blasting radiations from a too-near sun and able to disturb the fine dust by a flux of opposed electrical charges. So the scientists claimed, and they even explained the vaguely familiar shapes seen in the swirling columns as due solely to the product of the imagination, much as a man will see the faces and images in the leaping flames of a fire.

But no one had explained why several people could recognize the same image in the same column at the same time.

Dennison sighed as he entered the airlock and slammed the outer door. He waited until the pumps had filled the vestibule and, opening the inner door, stepped into the body of the vehicle.

The shell was just that, a heavily-insulated body containing cramped living quarters, a mass of instruments for scientific observation, and a small but powerful electric motor. Once inside he removed the cumbersome armour and relaxed in the faint breeze from a whining fan. Anders sat leaning against the controls sucking at an unlighted cigarette, and Hendris bit at his knuckles as he stared through the dulled vision port.

"Coffee?"

"Why not?" Anders stared at the geologist. "Come on, Junior, you heard the boss. Make some coffee."

"I—" Hendris gulped. "What are we going to do?"

"We'll talk about it," said Dennison, and forced himself to be gentle. "But first lets all have some coffee." He stared at Ander's cigarette. "May as well have a smoke too; you got any more of those, Anders?"

"Sure." The engineer threw a crumpled package towards the commander, "Help yourself."

Dennison nodded, shaking one of the little white cylinders from the packet and puffing hard until the treated tip glowed into life. Gratefully he inhaled the smoke and offered the packet to Hendris as he passed out the steaming mugs of coffee.

"It's a funny thing," said the engineer thoughtfully. "No matter how hot it gets I still like my coffee the same way."

"Habit probably." Dennison alternated between sips at his mug and drags on the cigarette. "I remember one time at Tycho Station, must have been ten years ago now, during the time of the old Mark 15s, remember them?"

"I remember them," said Anders grimly, and touched a scar on his check. "I was servicing one when I got this."

"Well, as I was saying, I—"

"For God's sake!" Hendris jerked to his feet from where he sat against the inner hull. "Do you have to talk such rubbish at a time like this?" He gestured towards the vision port. "What's going to happen to us?"

"Steady, Hendris," warned the engineer. "No sense in flying off the handle."

"You—" Anger twisted the face of the geologist. "If you'd done your job properly we wouldn't be in this mess. Instead of servicing the shell you were probably playing cards or drinking or something. I'll report you for this, you incompetent fool! I'll—"

"Shut up!" Dennison's voice cracked like a pistol shot in the confines of the cabin. "Shut up and sit down!" He glared at Anders. "That goes for you too!"

"But he said—"

"I heard what he said. Now forget it."

"Forget it!" Hendris shook his head. "I don't intend to forget it. Anders is to blame for this and I want him punished for it." He stared at Dennison. "You're the commander here, aren't you? Well, then, do something."

"I told you to shut up," gritted Dennison, and something in his eyes, or it may have been the way his big hands clenched into fists, reduced the geologist to stuttering silence. "Now, since you've mentioned the matter, and incidentally spoiled the first rest period we've had in more than twenty hours, we'll talk about it." He looked at Anders. "Report."

"Right-hand tread sheared and broken. No possibility of repair." The engineer shrugged. "I'd say that the links broke through metal fatigue. There's still a lot we don't know about the effects of this radiation on unshielded metal. Or it may have been the temperature variation, or a combination of both, or we may have passed through a patch of chemicals." He glowered at the geologist. "What didn't happen is that I fell down on the servicing. It's my neck too, you know."

"I know that; Anders, and no one is blaming you." Dennison shrugged. "The position is simple. The shell has broken down and we can't repair it, and so we must get back the best way we can."

"How?" Hendris didn't seem to be able to keep his eyes away from the vision port. "On foot?"

"Exactly."

"Are you insane?" The geologist turned and glared at the commander. "Do you know what conditions are like out there? Do you know what you're asking?"

"I know."

"But the temperature! It's over 650 degrees Fahrenheit, three times the boiling point of water; even lead and tin lie in molten puddles. And then there's the radiation! You don't know what you're saying!"

"I know what I'm saying," said Dennison quietly. "I've been on Mercury a little longer than you have, Hendris, about five years longer to be exact, which makes my stay here ten times longer than your own. I know all about the temperature, but the suits will enable us to stand it for a while, and as for the radiation—" He shrugged. "As we can't do anything about it, it's not much good worrying about it."

"A fool's philosophy," sneered the geologist. "Anyway, why can't we radio?"

"How?" Anders jerked his thumb towards the heavens. "With that static machine going full blast? And even without it we could only radio along line-of-sight. No Heaviside layer here, you know, to bounce back the radio waves."

"Then why can't we just stay here until they send help out from the Station?"

"How long do you think that will be, Hendris?" Dennison shook his head "We've been moving on an erratic path—along five degrees of arc. Even if they send out a search party now, and there's no reason why they should, it would take weeks to locate us." He nodded towards the air tanks and stores. "We've just about supplies to last us for another five days."

"They will find us before then."

"You think so?" He shrugged. "Personally I doubt it."

"But they must get worried about us," insisted Hendris. "They just can't send out a party and forget all about them. Someone must know what happened and do something about it."

"Look, Hendris," said Anders with exaggerated patience, "Mercury isn't Earth, you know. We can't keep in contact by radio, and yet the planet must be explored and charted. Normally there isn't any danger out on the day side, except from heat and radiation, that is, and the shell insulates us against those. It was sheer bad luck that the tread broke; just one of those things. I've been here nearly six years now and I've only known of one shell that failed to return within three days of scheduled time. Accidents normally just don't happen."

"What happened to them?" Hendris licked his lips with a nervous gesture. "The men in the missing shell, I mean."

Anders shrugged.

"They were never seen again," said Dennison quietly. "Their shell either. Vehicle and crew simply vanished." He rose. "But we won't vanish. We're going to get back to the Station."

"By walking?" Hendris didn't trouble to hide his sneer.

"Yes," said Dennison sharply. "Or do you know of a better way?"

"Not all of us need go," whispered the geologist. "One of us could stay behind, the supplies would last one man fifteen days, long enough for help to arrive from the Station." He looked pleadingly at the commander. "That makes sense, doesn't it?"

"It does."

"I suppose that you want to be the one to stay behind," sneered Anders. "Live it out in luxury while we sweat to get help. You yellow swine! Who the hell do you think you are?"

"Take it easy, Anders!" Dennison stared at the geologist. "Are you scared, Hendris?"

"Yes. Yes, I'm scared and I don't mind admitting it. The plain out there, worn to dust by countless years of heat and radiation. That sun, all swollen and looking as if it might burst open at any minute. The sand devils—" He swallowed. "Yes. I'm scared."

"No shame in admitting that," said the commander quietly. "I was scared when I came here first, and for just the same reasons, but it passed, Hendris, it passed." He shrugged. "Anyway, there's no point in arguing who is going to stay and who isn't. The answer is simple, no one can stay."

"Why not?"

"Listen," said the commander seriously, "we've more than sixty miles to cover and it's not going to be easy. We shall have to wear the suits all that time, go without food and make do with the water in the suit-bottles. Even with the low gravity to help us, the weight of the armour will still make it similar to travelling more than a hundred miles on Earth with full packs, and we've got the heat to put up with as well."

He paused, and in the silence the low purr of the air conditioner sounded strangely loud. Out on the grey plain, dimmed by the glare-shields over the vision port, the swirling columns of the sand devils seemed to be thicker than normal.

"We'll have to carry extra supplies of air, all we can manage, water too if possible." He looked at the engineer. "Can you cut the heat shielding from the shell, and would we be able to carry it as protection against the radiation?"

"We could, but it wouldn't be worth it. The insulation is heavy, it has to be, and carrying it would slow us down too much."

"I see." Dennison frowned. "I'm worried about the air. We'll have to carry it somehow."

"We could cut a skid sledge and drag it behind us," suggested the engineer. "Rig it for a two-man harness and take turns."

"Yes, we'll do that." Dennison sorted out tools from a locker. "Hendris, check your armour, make certain that your air and water tanks are full. Check your batteries too, there are Diracs in the rack." He looked at the geologist. "Remember, the next time you put that suit on you keep it on until we reach the Station. That may be a long time, and if anything goes wrong you've had it."

"I understand."

"Good. You do the same, Anders. I'll check my equipment after we've assembled the supplies and stripped the inner hull for the sled. We can weld it outside with the torch." He bared his teeth in frustrated anger. "Almost a full repair shop here, and we can't fix that tread. Damn it, Anders, why can't we?"

"No spares or replacement parts." The engineer shrugged. "I've warned them about it before, but they say the treads have all been tested to a hundred percent margin of safety. Theoretically, a tread just can't break down. They know that once a shell or armour is damaged it has to be repaired on the spot, that's why they send out an engineer with each vehicle but spare treads take too much room."

He grunted as a section of the inner hull came loose with a hiss of air escaping into the vacuum compartment between the hulls. Resting it on the floor he swiftly cut it to shape, welded ring bolts to the edges and nodded with approval.

"That should do it. Ready?"

"Yes." Dennison stepped towards the control panel and ripped loose the compass. "We'll open both doors of the airlock and Anders will pass out the sledge and supplies. Seal helmets now, and each check the other's armour."

Air whined from the interior of the shell as the doors opened on the grey plain outside, and together they stepped into the glaring light of the monstrous sun. Anders handed down the sledge and long, insulated tanks of oxygen and water, he followed with rolls of wire ripped from the drive mechanism of the shell. Carefully Dennison lashed the supplies to the crude sledge with the wire and fastened other lengths to the ring bolts. He handed one set of harness to the engineer.

"You pull with me, Anders," he said over the radio. "Hendris will walk ahead and watch for soft patches. You can take his place after an hour, and I'll change with you an hour after that."

"Two on one off, eh?" Anders chuckled. "Shouldn't we switch off radios?"

"Not necessary. The Diracs hold plenty of power, more than enough to last until we reach the Station, or—"

"Or until we're dead." Hendris swallowed, the sound echoing clearly through the helmets. "Let's get moving."

"Yes," said Dennison quietly. "Let's."

Slowly they began to move over the vast Mercutian plain.

CHAPTER 2

Lee Correy sat in a room and played chess with a man almost ten million miles away in space. A tall, dark-haired, broad-shouldered man, his features bore a striking resemblance to those that stared at him from the flickering surface of the visiscreen. Both had the same firm chin, the mobile mouth, the wide-spaced, deep-set eyes of midnight black. Both wore the trim uniform of the Spatial Service, the neat black and silver fitting snugly to their bodies, and both seemed to be about the same age.

But not quite.

There was a grimmer set about the mouth of Lee Correy, a tightening of the lips and a hardness of the eyes, missing in his younger brother. Responsibility had graven lines deep into the smooth surface of his flesh, and his calm, almost sombre, features lacked his brother's devil-may-care quirk of his lips.

"Bishop to QR8."

Lee nodded and moved a piece.

"Knight to Q9." He sat, his hands relaxed on the board before him, waiting for the almost two-minute gap before his brother could receive his message and the answer return. As he waited he listened, almost unconsciously, to the muted purr of the Mercutian Station. It was always there, the soft murmur of hidden machinery, the sough of the air conditioners, the chuckle of relays and the whisper of surging power. While the sound remained the Station was safe and the lives of every man on Mercury depended on the Station.

"Pawn to QB7." Jack grinned at his brother. "I hope that everything is all right down there."

"Rook to QK2." Lee nodded. "You've nothing to worry about. Just sit back and let the beam bring you in." He smiled, a rare thing, and his eyes were soft as he stared at his brother, "How does it feel to be a passenger, Jack?"

"Lousy. I'm used to bringing them in with these," he held up his hands, "not relying on a mass of radio tubes and relays. I'm not happy, Lee. Supposing something goes wrong?"

"Nothing can go wrong. The beam is simple and you know it. Just an extension of the aircraft radio control used on Earth for hundreds of years now. Just sit back and let science do the work."

"Yeah, and what if science blows a fuse?"

"You set in and land by manual control." Lee shrugged. "Relax Jack. Everything is as predicted. You're coming in on a tight beam relayed from the projector on the night side just over the edge of the libration area. When you get within three diameters the automatic control will take over for landing. It will do everything, check course, fire jets, spin ship, and set you down light as a feather. No possibility of error now, Jack. No human element to worry about. The beam control will make space flight as safe as stepping into bed."

"And make all pilots redundant."

"No, Jack. Pilots will still be carried in case of emergency." He saw the expression on his brother's face and changed the subject. "What are you bringing us this time?"

"More damn robots," Jack grinned. "A spare robotic beam control in case the one you have turns sour on you. Three professors who want to study the sunspots at near range. Ten men for replacements, a couple of crawlers for night side exploration, and the same amount of shell for daytime ditto. Personal armour, food, water, more food, recreational supplies, a little liquor, and a stack of mail as high as a house."

"Good."

"All of which you will pay for with a cargo of Diracs, small size, Asteroid Miners for the use of." He chuckled. "Seriously though, Lee, I'm looking forward to seeing you."

"And I you, Jack. Five years now, isn't it?"

"Five and a half, ever since they made you Commander of the Twilight Belt and lifted me to a Captaincy. Since then you've stayed put and I've roved the System." He sobered. "Don't you ever regret it, Lee?"

"No."

"Sure?"

"Very sure." Lee shrugged. "I've done my travelling, Jack. I've steered a spaceship to all the known planets and trod on alien worlds, but it was nothing like this. Here I'm doing an essential job. I've got two hundred men in my command, and the System depends on me to supply them with charged Dirac accumulators. We've a constant enemy here—the sun. We've a constant challenge—the night side. Boredom is something to be beaten and morale more than just a word. Mercury is on the threshold of becoming one of the most important planets in the entire System, and the beam landing control will end the bugbear of lost and crashed ships. No, Jack, I don't regret it."

"I'm glad to hear that, Lee. I'd thought—" Jack shrugged. "Tell me of your little empire, I've never been to Mercury before, you know."

"I know, and in a way it's lucky you didn't." A shadow drifted across the sombre features. "Too many ships were lost and too many men ended their lives in molten ruin or crumpled destruction. Mercury isn't a normal world, Jack. It doesn't fit into the nice, neat, Newtonian mathematics. It's an Einsteinian world. There are no straight lines here, there can't be, the terrible gravitational field of the sun warps very space and distorts normal geometry. Distances are deceptive, magnetic fields vary; the whole fabric of space-time is twisted to something alien and even yet not wholly understood."

"And yet you live there."

"Yes, Jack, men live here. They live in specially constructed domes, insulated against the terrible heat, self-contained and divorced from their surroundings. We live on a narrow strip in the centre of the libration, the Twilight Belt as we named it, a place where the heat of the day side and the cold of the night side meet and, to some extent, nullify each other."

"But the libration is almost forty-seven degrees of arc, twenty-three plus either way. Where do you get this 'narrow strip' business?"

"The libration is, Jack, and more than five hundred miles either side of the Twilight Belt are baked and frozen during our year of eighty-eight days. But we can't use those miles; one edge would put us too far on the day side, the other too far towards the night side. We have to use the ten-mile belt and spread our thermocouples and heat exchangers as far as we can."

"Somewhere I've heard this before," said the young man, and chuckled. "Sorry, Lee, but space pilots are supposed to know their planets."

"And Station Commanders their spaceships." Lee smiled and glanced at a chronometer, checking the time needed for his brother's answer. "Shall we finish the game?"

"Not now. I'll beat you later, when we don't have to wait so long between moves. 'Bye now."

"Goodbye."

The screen went dark, the image slowly fading as the connection was broken, and Lee sat for a long time before the instrument, staring down at the chessmen on the board before him, fighting for the hundredth time the nagging node of worry and doubt.

So much depended on the beam control.

In effect it was an electronic brain, sending out its invisible tentacles of radio impulses on a tightly shielded beam to a companion instrument aboard the spaceship. Together the two instruments would operate the ship, replacing human error and human reliance on the senses, with the cold, inhuman, logically correct current flow of matched relays and feed-back circuits. Relays would trip the firing controls of the approaching vessels, would spin it, adjust course, decelerate and land.

Without the vagaries of an atmosphere to complicate the workings of electronic computations, with nothing but course and speed and position to check and control, spaceships could land on Mercury without fear, safe in the infallibility of the beam control.

For there had been too many lost ships.

Lee shuddered as he remembered them. The vessels that had been piloted by human hands and human eyes and human brains. Some had crashed to splintered ruin against the frigid night side, others had careened towards the sun, to be caught in the tremendous gravitational field, their venturis spouting futile flame as they drove towards molten destruction. For on Mercury senses lied, things were not as they seemed, and even instruments were disturbed by the warping effects of Einsteinian space. Not even veteran pilots were safe.

Lee still remembered with sick horror the fate of old Captain Bridges who had first brought him to the Twilight Belt. For once the old man had made an error, trusted perhaps his eyes against his instruments, or perhaps trusted his instruments against his instinct. He had missed Mercury by a whole diameter, fully three thousand miles, and his voice as it came over the crackling radio had held horror and amazed disbelief. Lee had listened to that thin voice as it sped towards the waiting sun, listened to it until the growing roar of static had hidden the faint words, the radio distorted and useless by the radiations pouring from the Solar Furnace.

Sometimes, especially during the silent hours of his sleep period, he would awake in a cold sweat remembering those words—and now his brother was headed towards Mercury!

But it would be different this time. Now there was no more risk, no more cause for worry; there would be no more ships flaming like dying moths against the fury of the sun. Now Mercury would be open to the space lanes, and the modern magic of the beam control, sending out its radio impulses far from the day side, shielded by the bulk of the planet from the distortion of the sun, would serve as a guide and a beacon to the argosies of space.

There was no need to worry.

He looked up as a man knocked and entered the office, nodding at the casual salute and pushing aside the chessboard with its carved pieces arrayed in silent war.

"Yes?"

"Your pardon, sir, but one of the shells, number seventeen, has failed to return."

"How long overdue?"

"Two days, sir."

"I see." Lee frowned. "Number seventeen you say. That would be the one with Dennison and Anders. He frowned again. "Isn't there a third man?"

"Yes, sir. Hendris, a geologist, a new arrival. This is his first trip to the day side in a shell."

"Now I remember. Two days overdue is it?"

"That's right, sir."

"Return to duty. I'll be at the control tower if wanted."

"Yes, sir." The man saluted again, casually but with the respect every man on the Station felt for the sombre commander. Lee stared after him, feeling again the nagging core of worry and doubt, then sighed and, rising from his chair, left the office.

The control tower lifted its slender height a thousand feet above the grey plain, and from its summit could be seen the clustered domes of the Station, the ranked buildings of the charging sheds and the thousands of thermocouples and heat exchangers, aiming their great concave bowls towards the swollen glory of the sun.

Towards the frigid darkness of the night side rested the landing field for the too-rare spaceships. They came with their hulls stuffed with food and essential staples, and left with their holds full of the small but powerful Dirac accumulators. Past the landing field, towards the mysterious region of utter cold, cold approaching the absolute zero with temperatures of minus four hundred degrees Fahrenheit, lay the squat bulk of the beam control, its huge wirewed projector shifting slightly as it tracked the distant spaceship.

Lee stared at it for a long time, his eyes thoughtful, then sighed and turned towards the burning splendour of the sun, narrowing his eyes as he searched for the betraying glitter of a returning shell.

"You see them?"

A man entered the small, instrument cluttered room, and Lee smiled towards him. An old man, his uniform hung like a sack on his sparse figure and a mane of white hair tried unsuccessfully to hide a high, wide forehead. Pale, washed-out blue eyes held the glittering fires of burning intelligence, and his thin, claw-like hands quivered a little, a vibrating tremor of bone and sinew, almost as if vibrating to the pulse of hidden energies.

Despite his personal carelessness, Lee looked at the old man with respect. Doctor Carl Dirac was known throughout the System. He had spent twenty years on Mercury, arriving almost with the first ship, and during that time he had seen the Twilight Belt yield to the feet of man. From a single, poorly insulated dome the Station had spread and grown into what it now was, and that spread was solely due to the doctor's invention of the Dirac accumulator.

Due to him also was the squat bulk of the beam control, and the young commander sighed as he turned from the shielded window.

"Not a sign, Carl. Still, they're only two days overdue and Anders is a good engineer."

"To break down on the day side is bad," said the old man in his stilted English. "Maybe, when I have solved the problem of curved radio transmission, we won't have this worry."

"We wouldn't have it now if we had a jet scooter," said Lee bitterly. "It's ridiculous that we have to confine ourselves to ground transport the way we do."

"Ridiculous?" Dirac shrugged. "Perhaps. But while every ship must carry food and water for the men a scooter is a luxury we must do without." He gestured towards the beam control. "Later perhaps we can afford such things, but jet scooters require metals and machining we cannot do; they must be built on Earth and shipped here. Also, unlike the ground vehicles which can be powered by my little invention, they need fuel, lots of fuel, and with every second ship facing the danger of destruction and every third ship the certainty, fuel is something we must do without."

"Yes," said Lee quietly, and stared sombrely towards the burning plain. The old man was right. Cargo space was too precious to waste on scooter fuel. On a planet where every mouthful of food and drop of water had to be imported from Earth such things had to be done without. He thinned his lips as he watched the rising plumes of the uncanny sand devils.

"They are thick today," murmured the old man in his car. "Like I have never seen before."

"They're a nuisance," snapped Lee. "The instruments go haywire when they're around and the men don't like them."

"Perhaps not, yet to me they are interesting."

"They would be," agreed Lee. Strange foci of electro-magnetic forces, little whirlpools in the ether, an unstable balancing of opposed charges. He shrugged. "Harmless enough, but disturbing to a man with too much imagination."

"Perhaps, but where else in the System could they exist?" Dirac shook his head. "Only on this planet could they be born of the spatial stress surrounding the sun, and possibly only on an Einsteinian world." He fell silent, and for a while the two men stared at the shifting columns of swirling dust.

At the base of the tower the sand devils spun and writhed like clay on a potter's wheel. Strange shapes coalesced from the grey waste, odd phantoms of alien nightmare, a distorted man-shaped thing, a curved, smooth object, then, with startling abruptness the pluming columns met, joined, and both men stared at a replica of the beam control.

It lasted for as long as a man needs to take a breath, then it had gone, splitting into whirling columns, and each column raced towards the distant horizon, dwindling as they moved and vanishing in smallness and distance.

"Did you see that?" Lee stared at the doctor.

"Yes."

"The beam control! They copied the beam control!" The commander didn't seem able to believe his senses. "How could they do that?"

"Perhaps it was an accident, a coincidental joining of several fields to form a matrix on which the dust rested in a familiar shape. There could be any number of such fields and, eventually, they will resemble something familiar," Dirac smiled. "I remember when a boy I used to lie on the grass and stare at the wind-blown clouds of Earth. I saw many strange things take shape in the heavens, castles and dragons, spired cities and monstrous beasts, all woven from clouds and the fabric of imagination. Here, instead of clouds, we have eddies of vagrant current, the sand devils as we call them, but imagination needs so little to work on. A leaping flame—and you see a face. A cloud—and an army marches to war. A sand devil—and we see the beam control."

"Simple," said Lee sarcastically. "But I can trust my eyes and I know what I saw. Imagination or not, I saw the beam control, saw it as clear and as plain as though I'd been standing beside it. Dreams aren't like that; you don't see the mortar between the bricks of your cloud castles. You can't see the hairs and pores of the skin on a flame face. I tell you I saw the beam control just then, perfect in every detail, and you saw the same."

"Yes," said the old man slowly. "I saw it too."

"And do you really believe that it was wholly due to imagination?"

"What else could it be?" said the old man evasively.

"I don't know." Lee frowned and, closing his eyes, pressed his thumb and forefinger tightly against either side of his nose. "Perhaps you're right. Perhaps it is all due to imagination and accident. I wouldn't know." He stared out of the windows. "There is enough mystery on this planet without making more. There are enough unknown things hidden away on the night side, and on the day side too, for that matter, without us worrying more than we can help. But do you honestly believe that what we saw was just a figment of the imagination?"

"No," said Dirac quietly, then before the young commander could say more, the old man had turned and left the cluttered room.

Lee sighed and stared bleakly through the shielded windows.

CHAPTER 3

It was a track that could have been made by a snail. A giant, impossibly huge snail, a broad, wavering track smeared across the rolling wastes of the grey plain. It led from below the horizon, a shallow groove torn from the dust and it would remain there until the end of time or the hand of man wiped it away.

Three glittering figures moved at the head of the slowly lengthening groove, and the skid sledge behind them wiped away their shambling footprints with its own wide swathe. Slowly the figures moved, stumbling, falling sometimes, sprawling glittering, armoured limbs in the dust, and yet always dragging themselves upright again and continuing their painful, shambling progress.

Within the suits it was hell.

Dennison had lost track of time. He had lost every sense but that of blurred vision and red pain. Agony lanced through him, clawing at his flesh, rubbed raw by the tough fabric and metal of the spacesuit, softened by streams of perspiration, stinging with the salt from his own body.

Beside him, leaning heavily on the crude harness, Anders plunged grimly forward, the sounds of his breathing echoing horribly from the inter-suit radios. Together with the harsh, gulping breaths came another sound, a low, animal-like whimpering, broken by snatches of prayer and bouts of obscene cursing. Hendris, staggering like a broken robot as he marched before them, almost insane from the pitiless sun and the monotonous grey sand, forgetting that he wasn't alone, and spilling from his gaping mouth all the mind-twisted thoughts and vocal noises filling his tormented brain.

Around them the sand devils plumed, dozens of them, spinning and wavering like smoke ghosts, shifting and falling, joining and separating, keeping company with the stumbling men as if they had been outriders to some ghostly cavalcade.

Watching.

So Dennison thought, and thinking it knew it for the fantasy it was. Dust couldn't watch. Unbalanced electro-magnetic forces had no eyes to watch with, no brain to direct those eyes if they'd had them, no intelligence to register what they saw if they had eyes to see or brain to direct.

He grunted as something slammed against him, and stared, almost stupidly, at the glaring ball of the sun, searing bright even through the thick glare-shields. Slowly he realised that he had fallen, toppled to the plain and rolled, like some helpless monster, on his back.

"You sick, Dennison?" Anders' voice cut through the whining monologue of the third man.

"No, just all in." The commander made futile motions before he remembered the one and only way to regain his feet while wearing armour. Carefully he rolled, throwing his weight hard against the left side of his suit and drawing his left arm far beneath him. Frantically he jerked his leg, then rested, gasping with exertion, staring at the fine grey dust against his faceplate. Then carefully he drew up his knees lifting his hips until he almost squatted on his thighs. A heave and he was upright. A struggle and he had regained his feet. The engineer caught his arm as he staggered.

"Maybe we'd better take a rest, Dennison. I could do with one and Hendris is almost over the line."

"Yeah." Dennison found it hard to talk. "I think you're right. Call the nut while I unload the sledge."

He stooped over the lashings, undoing them and tipping the precious load from the sheet of curved, shining metal. Tipping it he made a small shelter, a tiny patch of shadow among the searing brightness, then watched as Anders collected the geologist.

"Hendris! Snap out of it, damn you!"

"—and the Lord spoke unto Moses and—"

"Hendris!" Anger and impatience echoed from the radio as the engineer grabbed at the armoured shoulder of the ranting geologist. "Time to rest, man. To rest! Can you hear me?"

"—for there is a thing which man shall not do—"

"For God's sake, man, snap out of it." Anders pounded the geologist's armour. "Didn't you hear me? It's time to rest."

"—so ye shall sow as—" The droning monologue altered and broke. "What?"

"Come over here, Hendris," said Dennison into the transmitter. "We'll rest for awhile, try and get a little sleep, we're all done up."

"Yes," Eagerness brightened the voice. "Sleep. I like to sleep. I have dreams then, wonderful dreams of ice and snow, of rain and the rippling of many rivers. Yes, I see fountains and the desert bursts into fair lakes and tinkling waters, and though I walk through the valley of—"

"Hendris!" Dennison forced himself to be gentle. "Come over now and lie down."

"Yes."

"Anders. Help him will you."

The engineer grunted, but guided the shambling figure towards the upturned sled. Together they sat in the shadow, the geologist falling almost at once on to his back, his faceplate staring up at the searing heaven

Hendris." Dennison shook the armoured figure then grunted with disgust. "He's passed out. Help me turn him, Anders, I want to check his air tanks."

"How are we doing for air?" The engineer watched as Dennison coupled a fresh tank to the suit supply and refilled the almost exhausted containers. He followed it by blowing water under pressure into the suit tank, then checking the gauges the commander gestured towards the engineer.

"Your turn."

"I asked you how are we doing for air?"

"I heard you. Turn around and let me refill your tanks."

"Why don't you answer me? Is it a secret?"

"It's no secret." Dennison watched the falling needle of the gauge and removed the empty air tank. He heaved it aside, coupling a fresh one to the engineer's suit. "I just don't know."

"How's that? You must know how much air we've been using and how much remains."

"Yes, I know that, but I don't know just how long we've been travelling or how much further we must go before we reach the Station." The commander closed the valve and uncoupled the tank. "Hold still," he ordered as the engineer shifted. "I want to fill your water container."

"Leave some for yourself," reminded the engineer. Over the suit radio came the sound of eager sucking as Anders drew water up through the flexible tube connected to the water container.

"Damn!"

"What's the matter?"

"I'm burned." Pain twisted the dim voice and the armoured figure heaved as it twisted around. Dimly, through the glare-shields, Dennison could make out the tormented features of the engineer. "My mouth is full of blisters, my chin is covered with them, and my throat—" The sounds of gagging came over the radio. "Damn it! That water was boiling hot!"

"Sorry, but you should have known. The container's been exposed to the direct sunlight for a long time now." Dennison turned his back. "Charge me up."

Tiredly he watched the tiny dials on the instrument panel just beneath his chin register the climbing amounts of air and water within his suit tanks. Anders grunted, and when he spoke his voice was a painful whisper.

"That finishes the water. We've one tank of air left, enough to charge two suits, but not three." He paused. "Are you certain that you've forgotten how long we've been travelling?"

"That's what I said."

"We should have had enough air," mused the engineer. "We took it all and there was enough to last us all five days. Have we been marching that long?"

"I don't know."

"But we should have enough air, shouldn't we?"

"We should, yes. Stop worrying about it."

Surprisingly, the engineer laughed, a wheezing crackle of difficult mirth, and Dennison could guess what pain the man must be suffering.

"You're a poor liar, Dennison. It might work with someone like Hendris here, but not with me."

"I don't know what you're talking about."

"No? I'll tell you then. Even though the air would have lasted us five days within the shell, it doesn't mean that it will last us that long now. The suits can't clean it as well as the shell air conditioners could. We waste too much by poor reclamation, the carbon dioxide builds up too fast and the suits can't freeze it out of the used air. I'll take a bet that we only have enough for three or four days at the most."

"What of it? We can cover sixty miles in four days."

"Can we? I doubt it. The dust slows us down too much. Another thing. We're losing too much water in the way of sweat. These suits were never designed for more than six hours operation at a time. We've been in them—how long? Sixty hours? Seventy? Maybe more. Whatever it is, it's a long time. I feel filthy, but I can stand that. I'm raw all over, but I can stand that too. What I can't stand is the thought that if something should happen to me I'd be helpless."

"How do you mean?"

"You know what I mean, Dennison. These blisters of mine, I can't even touch them, and I've got an itch in the centre of my back. There's nothing I can do about that either. I've just got to stand it, like a crab with a dozen lice crawling about beneath its shell. It's damn near driving me crazy!"

"Steady Anders!" Dennison frowned at the note of hysteria in the other's voice. He knew exactly how the man felt, for a long time now he had desperately tried not to think of a burning itch on his right thigh, and his face felt sticky and covered in filth from sweat and something that felt like blood but probably wasn't.

A spacesuit was more than protection against the heat and lack of air. It was a prison, the smallest prison ever made, and each man was cut off from all outside contact once the great helmets had been fastened down. Some men could stand it, others broke down with claustrophobia, shrieking madly for release and escape. No man could wear a suit for too long because, if for no other reason, no living organism can live in its own waste.

They had already worn the armour too long.

Dennison knew it, knew too that they would have to wear them until they died or until they reached the Station. They had no option, one way or the other, and he hoped that the ending would come soon.

He twisted, lying on his side, sheltering the suit from the direct glare of the sun in the dark shadow cast by the upturned sledge.

"Get some rest, Anders," he ordered. "You'll feel better after a sleep."

"Maybe." The engineer didn't sound too hopeful. "Look, Dennison, while we have the chance to talk privately."

"What?"

"Supposing we don't have enough air? Supposing that we have to use the remaining tank to charge the suits? What then?"

"We share three ways."

"And supposing that the Station lies just over the horizon when the air gives out? Three men would die then instead of one. You know what I'm thinking about?"

"I know, Anders. Forget it."

"But I can't forget it. This damn suit won't let me. I keep thinking of what I'm going to do when I reach the Station. I'm going to have a bath, I don't care how I get it. I'll dive in the supply tanks if I have to, then I'm going to sit in the refrigerator and get really cold. All the time I'm doing that I'm going to drink gallons of ice water, and while I'm drinking I'm going to scratch." He drew in a deep breath. "Then I'm going to enter the night side, get really deep into it away from the Twilight Belt, and I'm not going to stop until I see real ice and snow."

"Frozen oxygen and carbon dioxide, you mean. There's no water on Mercury."

"Maybe not, but it'll look all the same." Anders paused. "Then I get to thinking. What if the air runs out a mile too soon? What if we die within reach of the Station? Damn it all, Dennison why should we have to die because of a newcomer like Hendris? He's insane already, useless, a passenger—and we can't afford passengers, not now."

"Go to sleep, Anders." Dennison let some of his tired irritation sound in his voice "Go to sleep and don't talk like a fool. You know that you don't mean any of it."

"Don't I, Dennison?"

"No. You're tired and worried, in pain and physically exhausted, but I know you, and you're not the man to abandon a comrade. It's just talk. Forget it and go to sleep."

"Yeah. Maybe you're right at that. Goodnight, Dennison."

"Goodnight."

Dennison smiled as he closed his eyes. Habit dies hard, and even though there was no 'day' or 'night' on Mercury, yet still men greeted each other with 'good morning' and said farewell with 'goodnight.'

Still smiling he fell asleep.

He awoke to the sounds of unleashed hell.

A man screamed and another mouthed thick words redolent of pain. The sun blasted down from the midnight sky and sand devils danced and wavered all around like the crazed distortions of a drugged nightmare. He was hot, sweltering hot, his skin felt dry and his mouth filled with slime. Grit coated his eyeballs and fur covered his teeth. He swore, trying to shut his ears to the gibbering sounds from the radio, and fumbled with his lips for his drinking tube.

The water was hot, not boiling, but not far from it. He sucked up a mouthful, washing his mouth with the tip of his tongue then letting the precious liquid trickle down his throat. He swallowed, trying to ease the pain in his throat, took another drink, and squinted through the dust-covered glare-shields of his helmet.

Two figures warred in scintillating frenzy. They stumbled, striking with metal-coated hands, kicking with metal-shod boots, tugging at a long cylinder between them and moving with exaggerated slowness. Light splintered from them, the shifting reflections of the searingly bright sun, and as they battled they seemed to shimmer, to almost dissolve into pure light, looking as the ancient Gods must have looked as they waged forgotten wars on fabled Olympus.

Dennison's voice rang in his ears as he yelled into the radio.

"Anders! Hendris! What the hell do you think you're doing?"

A babble echoed from the inter-suit speakers. A sobbing, semi-coherent, almost hysterical shrieking, and mingled with it, muffled and droning, the thick voice of the engineer.

"He's crazy. Help me."

"You're not going to kill me," shrieked the geologist. "I heard what you were talking about and you're not going abandon me in this hell. I won't let you do it! I won't let you!"

"Hendris!" Dennison heaved himself painfully to his feet. "Have you gone mad?"

"No. I'm not mad, but you are. You must be. I won't stay behind I tell you! I won't!"

One of the two figures broke away, staggering through the thick grey dust lugging the long cylinder of the remaining air container. Dennison stared at it, not knowing who had won the strange fight. His radio crackled to the thick, pain-filled tones of the engineer's voice.

"Dennison! The fool's got the air!"

"Don't come near me," screamed the geologist. "I'll kill you if you come near me." He lifted cylinder poising it above his head, and Dennison wondered at the maniacal strength of the man. He halted, squinting through his glare-shield, and the engineer shuffled towards him.

"I woke up and saw Hendris making off with the air tank." He swallowed, the blister in his burned mouth making it seem as though he spoke through a mouthful of potato, and Dennison winced in sympathy. "I called to him, but he either didn't hear me or couldn't make out what I was saying. I tried to take the tank from him and he turned on me," Anders hesitated. "What shall we do, Dennison?"

"Hendris!" The commander forced himself to remain calm. "Come over here and don't be a fool. You know that one man can't charge his own tanks, he needs help to connect the couplings and you'll die when your suit tanks are exhausted if you try to run off."

"I heard what you were talking about," gritted the geologist. "You want to share this air and leave me behind to die."

"Don't be a fool."

"Am I?" There was a strange calm in the man's voice. "Did I dream what I heard?"

"Yes."

"Liar! Now I know I can't trust you. Stay there, damn you! Stay and rot!"

He turned, the cylinder still poised above his head, and his armour flashed in the sun as he shuffled through the dust. Around him the sand devils swirled in a medley of confusing patterns, drifting and leaping, spinning and leering, with half-formed faces, threatening with half-formed limbs.

"Dennison!" Anders' voice held more than just pain. There was terror there, and fear, and a strained desperation. "He's got the air! All the air there is! Unless we get it back we'll be dead within a few hours!"

"We'll get it back," said the commander grimly. "You tackle him from one side and I'll grab from the other. Watch for that tank."

Anders grunted, then moving like two shimmering robots they shuffled towards the distant figure.

Hendris knew what they intended, the inter-suit radio operated on a common channel and they could hear his slobbering breath as he tried to break into a staggering run. Quickly they followed him, forcing leaden limbs through the hampering dust, forcing tired, overstrained bodies to fresh efforts. Sweat poured from soggy skins and pain stabbed them as raw flesh rubbed into bleeding misery against the suits.

Slowly they gained on the scintillating figure ahead.

He turned as they drew alongside, and his breath rasped taut with fear over the radios. Clumsily he swung the glittering cylinder at the engineer, missed, and with incredible agility he sprang back as Dennison grabbed at him.

The commander swore and shuffled closer.

"Stand back!" Hendris almost gibbered with fear and terror. "I'll smash your faceplate. I'll—"

Anders lunged at him, almost tripped as the grey dust dragged at his feet, and before he could recover the geologist had swung the cylinder with maniacal frenzy. It glittered as it swung, shimmering in the searing light from the swollen sun, and Dennison heard the crash as it smashed against the engineer's helmet, the sound echoing from his radio.

He heard the crash—and something else.

A thin, high-pitched whining. A ghost sound, like a timid whistle, an extended sigh. Together with the sound came the clogged voice of Anders, almost screaming in desperation, and hearing the sound a red film dropped before the commander's eyes and hate washed the fatigue from his heavy limbs.

Light flashed before him, dazzling, shimmering, almost blinding him with reflected glory. He snarled, swayed, clawed at the nearing shimmer, and grunted as something smashed against his protected hands. He gripped, pulled, and swung the cylinder as if it had been a reed. Swung it full against the glare-shields of the geologist!

Again the transmitted sound of the impact. Again the frenzied screaming and the whistling rush of escaping air, faster this time, rushing from the broken faceplate into the void, whining as it gushed from the suit, carrying a thin cloud of steam as the moisture exploded into vapour, carrying also the life of the insane geologist.

Rapidly then he turned and fell to his knees beside the still figure of the engineer.

"Anders! Can you hear me! Answer me, man, are you all right?"

"The swine got me, Dennison." The thick voice was a whisper vibrating from the radio. "He tried to smash my faceplate, he missed, but he cracked it just the same."

"Let me look." Dennison turned the limp, armoured figure, and thrust his face close to his glare-shields as he examined the other's faceplate. A thin crack marred one corner, a thread-like line tracing its path across the dulled plastic. From it a thin plume of steam arose, steam and, incredibly, frost. Dennison bit his lips as he saw it, knowing the escaping air was freezing by expansion, while the moisture expanded into steam before it could free ye, expanded then dissipated into the void.

"Bad?"

"Just a crack. Are you losing much air?"

"Too much." Some of the pain left the engineer's voice and he stirred a little, struggling to sit up. Dennison helped him, supporting the armoured figure.

"Hendris?"

"Dead. I smashed his face plate, he died at once."

"You were too generous to the swine. You should have cracked it and let him die slow. Die as I'm dying." Anders coughed and his breath rasped as he gulped at the thinning air within the suit. "Luck," he muttered. "A crack, just a lousy crack, and there's nothing I can do about it. Nothing." He sagged, and the whining plume of air grew thicker as the internal pressure widened the rupture in the suit. "Dennison. I—"

"Yes, Anders?" The commander stooped closer as if mere distance could make any difference, forgetting his radio contact. "Anders!"

A sighing groan, a rattling sound, and the whining hiss grew louder, drowning the death sounds of the engineer. It faded, died, and as it died the armoured figure slumped and collapsed as an empty sack would collapse, limbs sprawling and bent at odd angles, sightless eyes glaring through fogged plastic.

It was over.

For a long moment Dennison stayed, squatting by the body of the dead man, then he sighed, and dragging himself to his feet stared around him. The air cylinder lay to one side of the doubled figure of the dead geologist, and he picked it up, ignoring the man who had caused the trouble.

It was only then it struck him.

He was alone, stranded on the Mercutian plain, with less than six hours air in his suit and an unknown distance to cover. He had a tank of air, enough to last a further twelve hours—but there was no way of feeding it into his armour!

Grimly he began to plod towards the horizon.

CHAPTER 4

They saw him from the top of the control tower. A tiny glitter on the edge of the horizon, flashing as it moved slowly over the grey plain, stumbling, falling, crawling beneath the glaring sun.

Lee heard the news as he sat in his office checking the routine reports from the Station, and within minutes he had risen in the tower elevator and was staring at the distant figure.

"Have you sent out for him?"

"Yes, sir." The man pointed to where a shell moved swiftly across the plain, throwing dust from beneath its churning treads. "I ordered the pick-up as soon as he was spotted."

"Good," Lee adjusted the focus of a telescope and stared through the dimmed lenses. "Only one, impossible to tell who it could be." He stared at the officer. "Have you tried radio?"

"Yes, sir. I put a beam on him, but all we got back is static and noise." The man hesitated. "Shall I make the connection?"

"At once."

Lee waited as the man aligned the cup-shaped antenna and threw a switch.

"Station Control here," the man droned into the radio. "Station Control, Answer please. Answer." He paused, and in the silence sounds spilled from the speaker, weak, almost lost in the blurring static, and listening to them Lee felt the hairs bristle on the base of his neck, and alien fingers crawled up and down his spine.

A slobbering whisper from the speaker. The sounds a man would make with a wide-open mouth and swollen tongue. A man who staggered in the last stages of exhaustion, a rasping, wheezing, wordless sound of animal pain and mental torment. Mingled with the droning whisper was a peculiar retching noise, a dry, lung-jerking sound, and hearing it Lee snapped sharp orders to the Control officer.

"Contact the shell. Tell them to advance at full speed. That man is out of air. Hurry!"

Swiftly the man obeyed the terse orders, his voice a controlled evenness as he relayed the instructions, and out on the plain the dust swirled higher as the churning treads spun fast on their driving wheels.

The old doctor entered the room just as the glittering shell drew level with the tiny scintillating point at the edge of the horizon.

"He has returned? That is good. It is a bad thing for a man to be lost on the day side."

"One has returned," said Lee grimly. "That shell had three men." He turned to the officer. "Contact the hospital and have them prepare for an emergency. Heat prostration, air lack and salt loss. They will know what to do." He thumbed the switch of an intercom as the officer muttered into a microphone. "Transport? Correy here. Have a repair shell go out immediately. I want them to backtrack along a trail and pick up a damaged vehicle. They can contact the trail by following the pick-up shell, which has just left. Look for two bodies also. I want full details as soon as possible."

"Yes, sir. Shall we dispatch two shells?"

"If you have them. Return with the bodies as soon as you can." Lee opened the circuit. "I'm going down to the Hospital, Carl, do you want to stay here?"

"No. I'll come with you." The old man stared at the shimmering dot of the returning vehicle. "That poor man," he whispered. "That poor, poor, man."

Lee nodded and led the way to the elevator.

An hour later he watched as men, moving with gentle care unsealed a suit of radiation blasted armour.

"We fed air into the suit as soon as we picked him up, sir." The commander of the shell stared pityingly at the armoured figure. "I tried to contact him over the radio, but couldn't make sense of the replies. I thought it best to leave him sealed until we returned."

"You did right," said Lee quietly. He nodded dismissal. "Report back to Transport Commander, there may be more work for you soon."

"Yes, sir." The man saluted and moved away, his armour flashing a little as he left the sterile room, and before he had taken two steps Lee had forgotten him, his attention riveted on what was happening on the table.

First the great helmet was unsealed and released from the neck clamps. As it came free a gush of stale, warm, odiferous air welled into the room from within the suit. Smelling it Lee felt nausea claw at the pit of his stomach, and he swallowed as he leaned forward to stare at the exposed features.

"Dennison," he murmured. "Now we know who is missing." He looked at the old doctor by his side. Dirac leaned forward from his hips, his pale, washed-out blue eyes betraying an immense pity as he watched the medicos strip the armour from the unconscious man. Watching him Lee remembered something he had once heard, something that had happened long before his time, and he understood why the old man should feel as he did.

"You were stranded once, weren't you, Carl?" He kept his voice low as the attendants lifted the limp figure of Dennison and carried it over to an operating table for examination. "How long was it before they found you?"

"Too long," said the old man sickly. "I was a fool, thinking more of my observations than of my personal safety, and I ignored the men who tried to warn me." He stared down at his quivering hands. "It was in the early days when everything was new and had to be explored at once. I'd gone off with a party deep into the day side, and we'd scattered a little but always kept within sight of each other." He looked al Lee. "We had no inter-suit radios then, you know, and it was important to keep within visual range."

"I know." Lee narrowed his eyes as the man on the table moaned and twisted a little.

"I had wandered off," continued the old doctor. "There was an interesting formation I wanted to examine, and after that another, and so on until I had gone too far. When I looked about me I was alone." He paused and swallowed a bitter memory. "The suits weren't what they are now, the insulation was poor and they only carried air for three hours At first I thought that it would be merely a matter of walking back the way I had come; I could follow my tracks: I couldn't get lost." He shrugged. "I did."

"But how? If you could follow your tracks it should have been simple."

"The sand devils," said the old man simply. "You know how they scoop up the sand and let it fall? Well, they had done that to me. Just a few footprints were covered, but it was enough, for we had travelled that area before and it proved impossible to pick out one track from another." He paused again, and now his hands trembled more than they normally did. "They found me just in time," he whispered. "I had begun to retch for air, my body was a blistered torment, and I was almost insane from terror. They found me and saved my life, but it was three years before I ventured into the day side again."

"And during those three years you perfected the Dirac accumulator, the one thing which has made it possible for us to double the normal wearing of armour and made it possible for men to wear spacesuits for long periods." Lee nodded. "A wonderful invention."

"No. A clever discovery perhaps—that much I will accept, but no more." The doctor shrugged. "After all, what is it? A container, strong and seamless, and within that shell a special combination of metallic chemicals arranged in a particular molecular fashion. Power is forced into that combination, torrents of power from thermocouples and heat exchangers here. That power is absorbed. It warps the atoms just a trifle, strains their relations to normal space-time, and so the power is held in a state of stability. Connect the terminals and the power begins to flow again, this time in reverse, forced by the strained atoms regaining their normal space-time position." He shrugged. "The accumulator is nothing but a sponge, soaking up electrical energy instead of water, and releasing it as required. A simple thing."

"Perhaps," said Lee drily. "But an accumulator the size of a man's clenched fist holds more power than any other type a hundred times as large. I wouldn't call such an invention a simple thing, the System owes it too much for that."

Dirac shrugged, then turned as a white-coated doctor straightened from the operating table and crossed the room towards them.

"How is he?" Lee glanced to where the medicos clustered around the unconscious man. "Will he live?"

"Just about." The doctor wiped his hands on a towel and flung it towards the disposal until; "He's in a bad way, there's no sense in denying it, but he should pull through."

"How bad is he?"

"Exhaustion, of course, and extreme chaffing of the skin—he's almost raw, but we can cure that. I'm more worried about radiation exposure and his mental health." The doctor looked towards where his men attended the sick man. "He was badly cramped when they brought him in, continual perspiring and loss of salt would account for that, and naturally he was in a mess. Luckily they got to him in time to prevent any serious lung lesions from air-retch, but he won't be fit for duty for a long while yet."

"Is he able to talk?"

"I've given him a hypo, it was essential he relaxed, and I'm putting him in a saline bath to lessen shock and to promote the growth of new skin." The doctor frowned. "Give him a few days, say three, before you try to question him, I'm worried about his mind more than anything else and he needs a long rest."

"I see." Lee sighed. "It seems as if we'll just have to wait. Look after him, doctor, Dennison's a good man."

"You don't have to tell me that. I remember the time when he carried a man more than five miles when he'd broken a leg and the shell wasn't due for two days. That was about four years ago, shortly after you came and before we had enough vehicles to go round. You remember the incident?"

"I remember it. The man fell from one of the thermocouples while on maintenance routine. I promoted Dennison to shell commander for what he did then." Lee smiled. "They were the good old days when we all had something to do and not enough time to do it in. You were kept pretty busy then."

"We were all kept pretty busy," chuckled the doctor. He fumbled for a cigarette, found one, and puffed it to glowing life. "When is the ship due?"

"Not long now, the last time I spoke with my brother they were five million out." He looked at the white-coated man. "You're due to go back aren't you?"

"That's right. I've done my hitch and it's me for the green hills of Earth." The doctor dragged at his cigarette and stared at its glowing tip. "You know," he said slowly. "I'll be sorry to leave the Twilight Belt in a way. This is a crazy planet, the kind of place the ancients must have had in mind when they talked about hell, but I like the people and I like the work." He grinned. "Must be getting old, and anyway, I've got work to do." He crushed out the cigarette, slipping the butt into his pocket, and Lee nodded to him as he walked away.

"I must get back to my work," said Dirac, and stared at the young commander. Lee shook his head.

"I'm staying here. The shell should be back soon with the bodies of the other two men and I want to examine them. I've reports to make, don't forget, and two dead men have to be explained."

"Perhaps they are not dead?"

"They're dead all right. If they weren't Dennison wouldn't lave come in alone. His tanks were exhausted and he knew better than to try and walk so far without carrying extra air. Anyway, if the shell had broken down so near he would have managed to send us word by the others, he isn't the sort of man to desert his friends."

"No." Dirac nodded. "He isn't. Until later then?"

"Until later." Lee slumped in a chair as the old man left the room and tiredly he puffed a cigarette to glowing life. He felt tired, his brain numb, and as he stared at the coiling streamers of blue smoke he thought over what the medico had said. Mercury was a crazy place and, on thinking it over, it fitted the description of hell perfectly. Both kinds of hell. The flaming pit of the later religions and the frozen, ice-bound regions of the old legends. Here they met in awful harmony, heat and cold, ice and liquid metal, blasting radiation from a swollen sun and the bleak coldness of the night side.

He nodded, surprised to find that he had almost fallen asleep, and jerked awake as men entered the room carrying armoured shapes of two limp figures. Quickly he stepped forward and stared down at the tell-tale faceplates.

"We found them a few miles from where they picked up Dennison," explained the shell commander. "His track wandered and he must have covered about twice the actual distance he travelled. There was an air cylinder full a short distance away from the bodies."

"I see." Lee stared thoughtfully at the splintered glare-shields on one suit and the cracked faceplate on the other. "Get these helmets off and strip the bodies." He stared at the medico. "Any way of telling which died first?"

"Not if they died within the same hour. Why, is it important?"

"It could be," said Lee grimly. "Two men dead—and they didn't smash their own faceplates. What does it look like to you?"

"Murder?" The medico shook his head. "Impossible!"

"Perhaps, and yet from the full air tank and the fact that they could have made it to the Station in comfort had they used it, something is wrong." He frowned down at the contorted face of the geologist.

"Death was instantaneous," said the medico quietly. "See how the surface blood cells have ruptured? The eyeballs? The congestion of the skin colouration and the signs of internal bleeding as the organs burst from lack of pressure? I'd say he went out when the faceplate was smashed, the air just blasted from his suit and the pressure dropping so rapidly that there was no time for internal compensation."

"I can see that." Lee stared at the dead eyes of the engineer.

"And this one?"

"I'd say he died slower than the other. The crack in his faceplate would permit the air to leak and so give him time to compensate for falling pressure." The medico pointed towards the blistered features. "Notice the eyes and lips?"

"What about those blisters?"

"Due to drinking boiling fluids. They were obviously done well before death."

"And you can't tell which died first?"

"No. They both died within the same short period, but it's impossible to even guess at who died first."

"Thank you." Lee rubbed at his sore eyes. "Strip their armour and put them in the morgue ready for cremation."

"Shall I cremate them at once?"

"No."

"But—"

"You heard what I said," snapped the commander. "I'm not going to repeat it."

"Yes, sir."

"That's better." Lee stared at the flushed face of the young medico. "For your information I'm not too happy about this, and until Dennison recovers enough to explain it, I don't intend destroying any evidence which may be needed later."

"I understand, sir, but it's impossible to even imagine Dennison murdering his companions. The whole idea is incredible."

"Maybe it is, but radiation does peculiar things to a man's brain, and these deaths must be reported and explained." Lee smiled at the young man's expression. "Call it routine if you want to, but believe me it has to be done. I've seen some peculiar things happen in space and on the planets, men, brothers even, have fought like animals over a can of food or a tank of air. I'm not blaming Dennison, but in all fairness to him this thing must be cleared up."

"Yes, sir. I'm sorry, sir."

"Forget it."

"Thank you, sir." The man hesitated. "I'll put the bodies in the spare compartment, the one next to the analytical banks for the beam control. Will that be all right, sir?"

"The beam control?" Lee frowned, feeling again a hint of his worrying fear, then shrugged. "Why not? They can't hurt the mechanism, dead men can't hurt anything." He nodded. "Put them anywhere you like and let me have your report as soon as possible. You know the sort of thing I want; time of death; manner of death; physical condition; brain lesions if any, and anything else you consider important." He smiled. "You know what the Brass Hats back home are like."

"Yes, sir." The man grinned, all his embarrassment and natural antagonism washed away by the young commander's shrewd understanding of his fellow men. Lee smiled, yawned, and rubbed again at his eyes.

"Space, but I'm tired! If anyone wants me I'm catching up on my sleep." He glanced at the dead men. "Nothing I can do here now, anyway."

He was yawning as he left the room.

CHAPTER 5

Jack Correy sat in the pilot's chair and glared irritably at the ranked controls. Around him the soft, pneumatic padding fitted his body with designed comfort, following the curvature of his body and ready to absorb the slamming weight of acceleration pressure. He had felt such pressure a hundred times, felt it as, with hands steady on the controls, he had operated the massed venturis, splitting the void with great streamers of blue-white flame, piloting the spaceship with brain and hand and eye, handling the massed weight with inborn skill and trained reflexes.

Now he was just a passenger.

Impatiently he stared at the luminous ball of the sun, huge and somehow menacing in the visiscreens, narrowing his eyes against the glare as he tried to find the small, almost invisible ball of Mercury against the too-bright background.

Next to him, lounging indolently in a padded chair, the astrogator chuckled with dry humour.

"Quit worrying, Jack. The electronic brain is doing all the work."

"Perhaps." Jack glowered at the humped casing of the beam control. "I don't trust that thing. Suppose something should happen at the last minute, what then?"

"Then you can do what you've been itching to do ever since we left Earth. You can grab hold of those nice shiny levers of yours and ride this tub down to the Twilight Belt." Seth Hammond pursed his lips as though he wanted to spit. "You've got nothing to worry about, ships will always have to carry captains and pilots, but astrogators—?" He shrugged. "Maybe I can get a job on Mercury."

Jack smiled.

"Things aren't that bad, Seth. It's different for me, used to handling the controls, not sitting here watching them bring moved for me, but astrogators never did have much to do once they'd plotted the course. I can't see how the beam control will affect you at all."

"No?" The thin astrogator glowered at the printed notice forbidding smoking while in space, and deliberately puffed a cigarette into life. Silently he handed one to the captain, then blew a streamer of smoke at the notice, watching the writhing coils expand, twist and vanish through the grill of the air conditioner.

"Everyone else smokes on this ship, so I can't see what difference it makes for the crew to join in."

"A hangover from the old days." Jack let smoke trickle through his nostrils. "A safety precaution against using too much oxygen. The Weimar conditioners fixed that, they could clean an old-time fog out of the air and not lose an atom of breathable gas, but they never got round to taking down the warnings." He grinned at the printed notice. "Or maybe they reckon it does morale good to be able to break a few rules now and again."

"Yeah." The astrogator glared at the humped machine. "I'd like to break a few rules. I'd like to take a hammer and smash that thing to junk."

"Why, Seth? It's only a machine."

"Sure it's only a machine, but so was the Spinning Jenny, and they had riots over that one. And what about the cybernetic clerking machines they introduced back in the last century? Remember what happened then?"

"Some men lost their jobs," admitted Jack. "But that was different."

"I'll say it was different. Some men lost their jobs, you say? Man, they had the biggest depression in history at that time. Haven't you ever heard of the Liberty Riots?"

"I've read my history. Local disturbances weren't they?"

"Local hell! Three nations had to declare martial rule and over fifty billion credits worth of damage were done before things quieted down." Seth breathed deeply through his nostrils, and his thin mouth twisted with inner bitterness, "Machines which replace personnel always cause hardship and trouble, and the beam control isn't any different in principle to the cybernetic clerks or the Spinning Jenny."

"Aren't you exaggerating a little?" Jack tried to keep his voice serious. "As I remember my history the cybernetic clerks replaced several millions of personnel. How many do you think the beam control is going to replace?"

"One is enough for me—as long as I'm the one," snapped he astrogator. "Look at the thing. Doing what you normally do, and what I'd be doing this moment if some jellyhead hadn't invented it. Damn it, Jack, are you blind? Can't you see what's going to happen when these things get widely used?"

"Sure. No more ships will crash into the sun."

"Be serious, can't you. I spent twelve years learning how to plot a course, twelve stinking years sweating it out at the Space Academy and worrying myself sick for fear that I wouldn't pass. I did, and for a while things looked rosy. A comfortable berth, good pay, and easy life, and then this has to happen."

"What of it? It only means that you can take things easy."

"It means that astrogators won't be wanted soon that's what it means!" Seth almost trembled with frustrated rage. "The damn things can lift a ship off planet, hook it on to a beam, and let it ride straight to its destination. It'll turn a spaceship into a trolley car and in time ship crews won't be needed, they'll just be too much extra weight."

"I think that you're wrong," said Jack quietly then, to change the subject. "How are the passengers behaving?"

"As usual. The three jellyheads are arguing over relativity again and the replacements are shooting dice against their future wages. The apology of a cook we carry is asleep as usual and the engineer's trying to convince himself that his girl friend meant it when she said that she'd wait for him." Seth crushed out the butt of his cigarette.

"Isn't it time you contacted the Station? We're getting pretty close."

"Plenty of time." Jack stared at the light-limned spot against the glaring sun. "We're still quite a way away yet. I expect the ship to spin and decelerate soon."

"See what I mean?" Seth kicked at the humped casing. "Normally you'd be checking distances and using your own judgment.

Suppose this thing has blown a fuse or something? How long do you wait before taking over?"

"While that light is on the carrier beam is being radiated from Mercury." Jack pointed to a green lamp set in the control panel. "An alarm rings and it changes to red if any thing should happen to the transmitter. The same thing will happen to a different lamp if baby here lets us down."

He picked up a scale and measured the apparent diameter of the sun, checking his reading against the gradations on the surface of the visiscreen, then took down a thick volume from a rack beneath the control panel.

"Let's see now. Apparent diameter is—" His voice died as he leafed through the pages of the almanac, finding out just how far the ship was from the Solar Furnace. "Mercury is about twenty-nine million miles from the sun therefore its apparent diameter should be—" He grunted as he measured the tiny disc of the black spot, then, noting the exact time, he set the figures on the keyboard of a small electronic calculator set into the panel.

"Checking up?" Seth grinned as he watched the captain determine the speed of the vessel.

"Why not?" Jack stared at the swinging hand of the chronometer, waiting until one minute had passed, then repeated his last observation. The difference in apparent diameter coupled with the elapsed time between observations gave to a fine degree of accuracy the forward velocity of the ship. He frowned as he read the answer to his equations through the plastic windows of the calculator.

"Well?"

The astrogator narrowed his eyes as he read the figures. "Fast." He stared at Jack. "Maybe too fast."

"Not really."

"Yeah?" Seth grinned. "I'll bet you ten to one that if this ship was on manual control you'd spin and start decelerating—"

Something clicked beneath the humped casing. Gyroscopes whined as current flowed to their motors, turning the ship on its short axis by reverse torque, and Jack smiled as he watched the stars move slowly across the visiscreen.

"Well, Seth? Still worried?"

The astrogator's answer was drowned in the shrill clang of an alarm, warning prior to firing the main drive. Five seconds later it was repeated, and again after the same interval. Jack strapped himself in the padded chair, rested his head firmly against the pneumatic cushions and waited for the pulse of thundering venturis.

They came as the whine of gyros died to a soft moan.

Sound vibrated through the spaceship, a drumming, surging, pulsating roar of unleashed power, quivering through the hull and vibrating from the bulkheads and stanchions. The snarling fury of the main drive transmitted from the gaping rocket tubes as flame spouted in blue-white fury against the coldly burning stars.

Weight slammed against him, pressing him deep against the padding, piling invisible tons on his chest and thrusting the flesh hard against his bones. It became difficult to breath, the effort needed to lift his ribs almost too much for his muscles, and he felt the strange, yet familiar numbness of high gravity acceleration creep over his body

Still the drumming of the rockets thundered through the ship as the blue-white exhaust streamed from the almost incandescent venturis. Ions, tiny particles of matter, heated and speeded almost to the velocity of light in the ravening heart of an atomic pile, flung from the vessel with incredible force and thrusting against the massed weight of the vessel in direct ratio to their own mass and speed. Their individual mass was small, yet lifted almost to infinity by their tremendous velocity, and their numbers were countless. So, thrust at the streaming fury of the miles long exhaust, the spaceship slowed its headlong velocity towards the menacing sun.

In the control room an alarm rang, and almost immediately the savage pressure died to a little above one gravity. Seth grunted as he rubbed the base of his neck.

"What was the idea of that?"

"Course correction. We were going too fast and the beam control cut our velocity down to what it should be."

"I know that, but did it have to do it all at once? Another couple of gravities and you'd have had to scrape me off the padding."

Seth grunted as he lit a cigarette. "That's the trouble with machines, no regard for human feelings."

Jack smiled and switched on the communication plate.

It took a little time for the tubes to warm. A little longer for the carrier wave to ride along the beam to Mercury and return from the Twilight Belt, but they were close now, very close, and the gap between question and answer had been cut to a matter of seconds.

Lee stared at his brother from the flickering surface of the visiscreen.

"Hello there, Jack. Everything under control?"

"You should know. Didn't you spot our exhaust?"

"Yes, what happened?"

"The beam control decided we were travelling too fast and did something about it in a hurry. It's all right now, though."

"Good. Nervous?"

"A little," admitted the captain. "I'm used to bringing them down myself, and I miss the feel. Guess after this trip I'll be out of a job."

"I doubt it." Lee hesitated. "I had a radio from Earth. It seems they are in a hurry to stock up with charged Diracs, something to do with the Asteroids, and they've sent out three more ships along the beam. It looks as if we're going to do lot of entertaining soon."

"Three ships?"

"Yes." Lee frowned as he stared at the image of his brother. "I wish they had waited. The beam control is still new, untested, and if anything goes wrong—"

"What can go wrong? Anyway, I'm carrying a replacement unit just in case."

"I know, and that's why it's so important you reach here safely, those other ships are depending on following the beam."

"Why? Aren't they carrying pilots?"

"Yes, at least I suppose they are, but you know the death rate of ships trying to land here." Lee smiled, a strained, almost painful distortion of his lips. "I must be getting old or something. The last time I felt like this was when mother died in that stratoliner crash over the Pacific." He shrugged, a circular movement of his shoulders as if trying to shake off the invisible burden. "Still, you're not a fool, and if the worst should happen you can always land on manual."

"You sound like an undertaker." Jack deliberately grinned and closed one eye. "What you need is some cheerful company. Wait until I get there, we'll break out the liquor and make drinking history. Nothing like good old alcohol to chase away the blues, and brother, you've got 'em bad."

"Perhaps you're right." Lee shrugged again. "I'll watch you on the radar. You're getting very close now and should touch down soon." He smiled. "Take care of yourself, Jack."

"Sure I will, and get rid of that depression."

Lee smiled again, a tired, despondent smile, and his image faded as he cut the connection. Seth grunted.

"I wish I had a brother like that," he said wistfully. "It must be nice to have someone worrying about you."

"We've always been pretty close."

"Then you're not like some brothers I know. Most of them seem to want to cut each other's heart out."

"We've always been pretty close," said Jack shortly. He stared at the thin astrogator. "Why don't you get married, Seth?"

"Married! You think I'm crazy?" The astrogator shuddered. "I remember a friend of mine got married once. We'd served together on the Venus-Earth run and he got married to a blonde he met in a dive near the spaceport."

"What happened?"

"She turned all respectable. Made him resign and settle down. The last time I saw him he had five kids, round shoulders, a load of debt and no hair." He shook his head in exaggerated solemnity. "Me? I want to enjoy life before I die."

"Then—" Jack stiffened, letting his words die into silence, and jerked to his feet staring at the astrogator. "Seth! The drive is cut! What—"

Sound shrilled through the control room, the steady screaming of an alarm, and even as the captain thrust at the cut-out switch he heard the astrogator's startled shout.

"The beam control! The damn contraption's let us down!"

On the panel, where a green light should have shone with quiet steadiness, a flaring red lamp flashed with soundless warning, and watching it Jack felt the twin stirrings of danger and excitement.

The beam control had broken and they were no longer connected with the electronic brain at the Twilight Belt.

He had to land the vessel on his own.

CHAPTER 6

It was soft green, smooth, dimly lit and without highlights or shine of my description. For a long time Dennison stared at it, lying like a thing of wood on the soft hospital cot, not really conscious of his arms and legs, not even thinking of turning his head, just lying, staring at the expanse of dimly-lit green while within his skull thoughts and dreams, memories and fantasies mingled in a weird, almost fairy-tale world.

There had been a grey plain—or had there? There had been shining knights in shimmering armour fighting with a gleaming lance—or had there? There had been swirling devils with changing faces and gibbering mouths, mocking and deriding, watching without eyes and muttering without mouths—or had there?

He didn't know—and, lying restful on a bed that felt like a cloud, he didn't care.

Slowly he became aware that the soft green expanse must be the ceiling, that the bed on which he lay must be in a hospital, and that hospital must be in the Station. With awareness came pain, the knowing ache of overstrained muscles, the burning soreness of healing skin, the sick throb of subcutaneous radiation burns, and with the pain came memory.

He knew who he was, what had happened, and what must have taken place, and knowing relaxed, smiling and devoid of all worry and doubt.

He was safe.

Sounds came to him then, the soft, familiar purr of the Station, the throb of hidden power and the sigh of the air conditioners. Those sounds were normal and, after living with them for more than five years, he would have felt uncomfortable had he not heard them. But mingled with the same familiar sounds, came the whisper of something else, something unfamiliar, and listening to it he felt his senses sharpen and his ears strain.

A sigh, a soft exhalation of trapped air, then a thud, dull and soggy. A scrabbling sound as though a great spider were trying to climb a smooth wall, and falling back with threshing limbs. A faint creaking as of rusty joints, and a snapping of stiffened vertebrae. A staggering, uncoordinated suggestion of clumsy motion, and a shadow, thin and faint, a mere darkening of dimness, moving oddly across the ceiling.

Dennison stared at it, feeling a sudden chill, a primeval tingling and a twitching of the muscles around his mouth a though his lips wanted to bare his teeth in a warning snarl. Fear touched him, a ghostly relic of a spectre-haunted ancestry, and for a brief moment civilised materialism fought primitive spiritualism, fought—and won.

He sat up on the narrow cot.

A man passed by the foot of his bed. A thin, emaciated looking man, with puffy features and eyes glassy, streaked with red, protruding almost from their sockets. The mouth sagged, the tongue lolling from open jaws, and he moved as an old man might move, as a person crippled with rheumatism or someone who had forgotten how to use their limbs.

Silent he was, deathly silent, and he passed like a thing from out of time and space, stumbling rather than walking through the quietness of the little ward with its sole occupant, staggering as he reached the far door, shuffling through it, out of the ward and into the room next to where the great electronic analysis banks of the beam control rested in their metal housing.

Dennison watched him go, staring with wide eyes, feeling his heart accelerate within his chest until it thudded with actual pain against the cage of his ribs. Within his skull thoughts raced like poisoned rats down the corridors of his mind, like snarling, red-eyed, gape-jawed rats, and as they raced they gnawed at the very foundations of his sanity.

Oblivion came then, came with a screaming darkness and flash of red and black, and as he fell back to the pillow so did his mind fall back down the years as he struggled to escape what he knew could not be.

And screaming, he died.

Lee heard the screams. He heard them as most men in the station did, and before the first echoes had died he was racing wards the hospital and the tiny ward where men near death were kept in peaceful isolation.

The doctor met him at the door, and a couple of medicos thrust past, hypodermics in their hands, running as they approached the bed. Before they reached it the screaming ended, cut off on a high note, finishing with savage abruptness, and they stood, helpless against the final enemy.

"What happened?" Lee caught the doctor by the arm. "What made him go off like that?"

"I don't know." The white-coated man stared sombrely at the twisted figure on the bed. "He shouldn't have died, there was no immediate danger, and if he was kept quiet and rested he should have pulled through." Automatically he puffed a cigarette into life. "From the look of him I'd say that he had a tremendous shock. You could almost say that he was literally scared to death. But how? Why?"

"That's your job." Lee pressed his thumb and forefinger tight against either side of his nose. "You know what to do and now that he's dead you may as well cremate the other two bodies." He glanced at the medicos. "Better do it now, we've kept them too long already."

"Yes, sir." The two men walked from the ward and into the room where the bodies had been kept. Lee heard then pause, the shuffle of their feet, and then shoes thudded on the floor as they came running back.

"One of the bodies has gone, sir!"

"Gone?" Lee glanced at the doctor, and the man shook his head.

"Impossible! I've been on duty in the annexe and no one carried a body out while I've been there. It isn't in here either." He stared at the two men. "Is it in the beam control room?"

"The beam control!" Lee swallowed as the old worry leap into sudden flame. "Let's take a look."

He was almost running by the time he reached the far door.

They found the body.

It lay, limbs sprawled in wild abandon, against the smooth metal of the housing, and as Lee stared at it he felt a quiet alarm. Someone had tampered with the electronic mechanism. An inspection port had been slipped to one side, and a fine mesh of transistors and silvery wires gleamed through the open panel.

"This is insane!" The doctor stared down at the dead man, and annoyance twisted his mouth into ugly lines. "Look! This was Hendris, he's been dead for days now, and yet from all appearances he got up from his slab and walked in here."

"This isn't humorous, Doctor," snapped Lee. He pointed towards the open inspection port. "Someone came in here, removed the body, tampered with the beam control and left the body lying as we see it." Anger tightened his lips into a thin line. "Fetch Doctor Dirac at once. Too much depends on this control to have any sympathy with the joker, whoever he may be, and when I find out who did this he'll suffer for it."

"Are you accusing me?" The doctor stepped forward, his cheeks flushed with anger. "I've already told you that I was in the annexe for the past duty period. I tell you that no one passed me at all."

"No one? What about Dennison? Who attended him?"

"I did."

"Personally?"

"Yes."

"I see." Lee stared coldly at the doctor. "So you admit that you are the only man who entered either of these three rooms during the past duty period. Do you realise what you are saying?"

"I only entered the ward, not the other rooms, why should I?"

"I'm asking the questions, Doctor, not you. If what you say is the truth, then you are asking me to believe the impossible. If you are asking me to credit a man several days dead with the ability to rise from his slab, enter this room, swing aside that inspection port—and then drop dead again."

"I'm not asking you to believe any such thing. I don't know how the dead man came to be in here and I'm not going to guess. All I'm certain of is that I had nothing to do with it."

"Then who did?"

"Damn it, Lee! Are you trying to say that I'm a liar?"

"No, Doctor, not yet anyway." Lee sighed. "But what am I to think? If anyone shifted that examination port it must have been you. I checked the equipment a few hours ago and every thing was all right then. The dead man couldn't have done it, and we know that Dennison didn't. What is the obvious conclusion?"

The doctor shrugged and thrust his hands deep into the pockets of his white coat.

"Make your own conclusions. Am I under arrest?"

"No. There's no need for it, not yet anyway. I'll have a guard in this room." Lee shook his head. "I can't believe that any man would deliberately tamper with the beam control, and as for the dead man—" He frowned and looked up as the old doctor entered the room.

"Trouble, Lee?"

"I'm not sure yet, Carl. Check the control, will you, I've reason to suspect that it may have been tampered with."

"Tampered with!" Dirac stooped over the humped casing and his hands trembled even more than normal as he slid aside the inspection ports and peered at the mass of complex wiring inside. He grunted and, twisting his head, peered at the young commander.

"Why did you turn it off?"

"I didn't." Lee stepped quickly towards the old man. "Isn't it working?"

"No."

"But—"

"You wouldn't have known from a casual glance, after all there are no moving parts and this part of the system has no warning light. No need for them really, the analytical bank should never be free of current flow." Dirac pursed his lips. "I don't understand this. Theoretically the analytical banks just couldn't go dead. There are two sources of power and the current amperage is extremely low. It just doesn't make sense."

"The ship!" Lee clawed at the old man's shoulder. "Carl! What about the ship?"

"As far as I can make out the carrier beam is still operating," said the old man. "It's only the banks which aren't working." He stared at the young commander. "You must cut the beam connection, Lee. Break it and warn the vessel. If you don't they will still think that the control is operating and they will be trusting inert metal to land the ship. You can guess what will happen."

Lee nodded, feeling his old worry mount within him, and stared sickly at the inert mass of the beam control. Without it the ship would continue on its present course, the vessel-unit waiting for flight instructions which would never come, and the men within it would never know what had happened until they piled in ruin or drove headlong towards the sun.

It took too long for the visiscreen to warm and the flickering surface to steady into a recognisable pattern. Impatiently he waited, his fingers drumming on the edge of his desk, and while waiting snapped brief orders into the intercom.

"Radio? Cut the beam control carrier wave. Cut it at once!" He threw other switches. "Observation? Track the approaching vessel with everything you've got. Radar, direct vision, light impulses, everything. Understand?"

"Yes, sir." The voice hesitated. "Trouble?"

"Perhaps."

Lee stared at the steadying surface of the visiscreen.

"Jack! Listen. I've cut the carrier wave, you may have noticed it by now."

"I've spotted it." Jack stared hard at his brother.

"Trouble?"

"Yes."

"The beam control?"

"What else." Lee shrugged. "Never mind that now. The only thing you need worry about is to bring the ship down on manual. Ignore the beam control, act as though you'd never heard of it, just land as you would have done normally."

"I get you, Lee." Jack smiled. "Don't look so serious. I've landed ships before, you know."

"Not on Mercury, you haven't. Now listen. Don't be fooled into thinking that it's easy, it isn't, and one out of every three ships don't make it. I'm quoting statistics. Jack."

"The odds are on my side, Lee."

"Don't kid yourself. We can predict that one third of the ships sent to Mercury don't make it. Of the rest it's a gamble whether or not you set down in one piece. I'm serious, Jack."

"I believe you."

"Good. Now it's up to you, but remember where you are. This close to the sun strange things happen. Light doesn't behave as it should and distances are deceptive. You can't even rely on your instruments." Lee hesitated. "I'm remaining in contact until you land. The rest is up to you. And Jack—"

"Yes?"

"Be careful."

"Sure. Don't worry now, everything's under control." Jack nodded towards the astrogator. "Right, Seth, we're on our own. Give me distances and speed. Quick!"

He settled himself in the padded chair and stabbed his thumb at the warning alarm, holding it down as the pre-blast siren wailed through the ship. Seth swore as he checked his calibrated scales.

"Something funny here. I'm getting two readings."

"How do you mean?"

"The apparent diameter of the planet is variable. If I'm to believe one set of figures we're heading away from it."

"That's impossible.

"I know, so we'll use the others." The thin man gnawed at his lower lip. "Better cut velocity some more, Jack. We're almost within two diameters."

"Six thousand miles!" Jack reached for the firing levers and weight slammed him hard against the padding of his chair. Desperately he kept the drive blasting at a nine gravity thrust, fighting the pain and ebbing tides of blackness lapping at the edges of his vision. Dimly he heard someone shouting, cut the drive to three Gs.

"Let me take another reading," yelled the astrogator. "I've been watching the screen and the damn planet is moving all over the heavens." He swore as he used scale and calculator. "Still two diameters. If I didn't know better I'd say that we were standing still."

"Maybe we are, that blast could have negated our sunward velocity." Jack stared at the searing glory of the swollen sun, narrowing his eyes as he stared at the round, black ball of Mercury.

It loomed large on the flickering surface of the screen, clean cut, like a piece of black paper pasted against the sun. Even as he stared at it the outlines seemed to waver, to shift a little, to shrink and swell with strange pulsing, the direct effect of the tremendous gravitational field surrounding the tiny world, bending light as water bends a sunbeam, and distorting what should have been a stable image. Abruptly the image jerked towards them. Thunder drummed through the vessel as Jack slammed at the controls, and blood rilled from the broken blood cells in nose and ears, from eyes and mouth as the terrible force of twelve gravities drove against yielding flesh. Dimly, over the snarling thunder, he heard someone calling his name, then ignored it as he concentrated on the jagged blackness looming below.

They were travelling too fast.

He knew it, knew too that there was nothing he could do about it except what he was doing, and he forced his hand to move the control another notch, piling a little more weight against overstrained flesh.

Ten seconds he waited, twenty, thirty, then just as the rising tides of blackness threatened to overwhelm him, he cut back the rocket drive.

Beneath the ship Mercury moved in midnight splendour

"Jack!" Seth wiped blood from his face and his finger danced over the keys of the calculator. "We haven't matched orbital velocity yet. The damn planet's running away from us."

"Can't worry about that now." The captain thinned his lips as he glanced at the wavering needles on the ranked instruments. "Stand by for extra blast."

Again the roaring thunder of the venturis vibrated through the vessel as the captain desperately slowed their velocity. He grunted as he watched the swinging needle on the radar altitude dial, noting the way it jumped and bounced, sure sign of mountains and deep gulleys. Next to him Seth groaned in impatient helplessness as the deceleration thrust him deep into the padding.

Something struck the hull.

Immediately Jack cut the drive to a throbbing murmur and grinned triumphantly at the astrogator.

"Made it! I'm balancing in stasis now and all we have to do is rise a little and set down on the Twilight Belt."

"Yeah?" Seth glowered at the dark surface of the visiscreen. "What was that which hit us?"

"Probably the summit of a mountain or an outcrop of rock. Felt as though it scraped a fin to me." He adjusted a control. "We'll ride on the jets until we can see what's happening. Cut in the ultra-violet filters on the screen, Seth, the infra-red won't be much use on the night side, not enough heat down there to warm an icicle."

"Don't forget the orbital vel—"

Sound echoed through the ship, a harsh, grating sound, and the structure vibrated to the impact of a mighty blow. Seth yelled as he stared at the ghostly surface of the visiscreen, flaring with the cold blue radiance of ultra-violet registration, and Jack swore as he grabbed at the controls.

Too late!

The ship tilted, rocked, and swung from the vertical. Rock tore at the metal of the hull, and men shouted in desperate frenzy from the lower sections of the ship. On the instrument panel needles flickered on ranked dials, and the soft pulse of the rockets died into whispering silence.

For a moment the ship seemed to hang poised, swaying a little, filled with soft murmurings from yielding stanchions and the shrill, complaining noise as metal grated against rock. Then, slowly at first, then with increasing speed, it fell, rolling down the side of the mountain against which it had struck, rolling and bouncing like an enormous tin can. Faster it fell, faster then, with a horrible medley of tearing metal and screaming men, of scraping rock and lurching confusion, it jammed against a towering mass of glittering ice.

Silence fell within the vessel. A murmuring silence filled with tiny sounds, mute and peaceful by comparison with the fury of the impact. The chuckle of still-operating instruments, the soft, piti-ful moaning of injured men, and over all the other sounds, shrill and whining, monotonous and insistent, another sound, master of them all.

The thin hiss of escaping air.

CHAPTER 7

They stood in line like grotesque monsters, each man in his armour, standing in the huge vehicle shed by the side of their crawlers. Strange vehicles these, like the shells used for the day side exploration in their self-contained cabins, but with wide, external treads and mounted with batteries of searchlights and thermal units. From each cabin the thin whip of a radio antenna lifted its slender height, and the squat muzzle of a flare cannon looked like an old-fashioned mortar.

Lee passed slowly down the line, checking each man's equipment and, as he passed, the crawler crews entered their vehicles and waited in readiness for the signal. Five of them, each crawler holding three men, and the group consisted of every night side vehicle on the planet.

Dirac crossed the wide, echoing shed and Lee turned as he approached.

"Anything new, Carl?"

"Nothing." The old man hesitated, staring at the vehicle. "Do you think this is wise, Lee?"

"What else can we do? We know that the ship crashed on the night side, I followed it down until it dropped below the horizon, and Observation managed to get a rough fix of its position."

"And what a position!" Carl shook his head. "More than thousand miles from the Station, deep in the night side, a region which we haven't yet explored. It's a hopeless task Lee."

"But one we must undertake." Bitterness dragged at the corners of the young commander's mouth. "If we only had a jet scooter it could find the wreck in no time, but we haven't and so must do it the hard way." He smiled the old man, a tight smile and one without humour. "I'll put you in command while I'm away. You know the Station better than any man, and you know what to do."

"Yes, Lee, but must you go?"

"The beam control is wrecked, God knows how or why and three ships are heading towards Mercury relying on it. Unless we find the wreck and the spare component the ships will crash into the sun or follow my brother into ruin on the night side."

"But it would have been smashed in the wreck!"

"We don't know that. Electronic equipment is pretty tough and it would have been packed well. Anyway, we must take that chance, and I'm going out to find it."

"Why you, Lee? There are other men just as able. Captain Weston. Hughes, Blain, a dozen experienced nightsiders. Need you go at all?"

"I can't stay here, Carl," Lee said quickly. "Not how things are, not while Jack may be lying out there, injured perhaps, waiting for help." He gripped the old man's arm. "Wish me luck, Carl."

"You know that I do," whispered the old man, and stood watching as the young man lifted himself into the cabin of the leading crawler. Slowly the great inner door of the airlock swung open, closed over the lead vehicle, and air whined as the vestibule was pumped empty of the precious gas.

One after the other the five crawlers, their wide, external treads clanking over the floor, entered the airlock and passed out into the airless mystery outside.

Carl sighed and turned away.

It was at times like these that he felt his age. Felt that perhaps he no longer belonged on the Twilight Belt, and as he made his way slowly towards the Control Tower his shoulders were stooped and the quivering in his hands had increased to an uncontrolled shaking.

Twenty years he thought bitterly. A whole generation he had wasted on the tiny ball of the hell planet—probing and worrying at the secrets of nature, trying to fill one more gap, solve one more problem in the great field laboratory which was Mercury.

And for what?

He had invented the Dirac accumulator, and that single thing would have made him the richest man in the entire System, but he had given it to humanity, retaining only a token royalty in order to pay for expensive equipment shipped from Earth, equipment that the Spatial Service couldn't or wouldn't supply. He had designed the suits, which permitted exploration of the searing heat and frigid cold of the day side and night side. He had designed the beam control analytical banks, the electronic brain, which was meant to guide vessels across the limitless voids of deep space, and thinking of it his thin lips twisted in self-contempt.

It had failed.

It had broken down at the moment when most wanted and a ship had crashed to destruction amid the airless wastes of the night side. Now Lee had gone in search of it, trying to do the impossible in a frantic race against time so the other ships could avoid the same fate. But if the beam control could fail once, then it could fail again, and he would have been responsible for them all.

He frowned as he thought about it, letting his keen brain work on the problem of why a mechanism designed never to fail had suddenly become so much inert metal. He was still thinking about it when the elevator hissed to a stop at the summit of the tower.

Far below, looking like ants as they crawled over the great plain, the five vehicles moved steadily and swiftly across the Twilight Belt and away from the sun. Carl stared at them, then glanced towards the Control Officer.

"Are you in contact?"

"Yes, sir," The man gestured towards the radio. "You wish to speak with the Commander?"

"If you please." Carl wailed until the man had plugged a handset, then spoke softly into the mouthpiece. "Lee? Carl here. How are things going?"

"As expected, I don't expect any trouble for quite a while yet. Still worried?"

"A little," admitted the old man. "What are your plans?"

"I'll set up a base camp as far forward as I can get. Leave a crawler there and take the rest deeper into the night side. I want to set up a chain of radio relays so that we can maintain contact over a wide area. We know roughly where the ship must be so it will only be a matter of quartering until we find it."

Static blurred the voice a little, then died as the commander spoke again.

"I've got Weston and Blain in the lead crawler with me. Both are experienced on night side conditions and we shouldn't run into trouble. Anyway, there's no option we've just got to get that component."

"I've been thinking about that, Lee. Have you any idea as to why the control should have failed when it did?"

"None."

"Nor I," admitted the old man. I'll sign off now; you'll be below the horizon soon now and out of contact. Good luck."

"Thanks." The voice blurred as it died into silence, and the old man slowly replaced the handset. Outside the sun threw the silhouette of the tower in deep black, clean cut lines over the plain, and at the edges of the shadow the pluming columns of the sand devils spun and wavered in their normal frenzy. He stared at them for a long time then, knowing that he could do no good in the tower, he made his slow way towards the elevator and down to the tiny hospital.

The doctor nodded a greeting at him as he entered the annnexe and held out a packet of cigarettes.

"Have one?"

"No thank you." Dirac shook his head. "I never got into the habit, but don't let me stop you."

"You won't." The man puffed a little white cylinder to smouldering life. "I hear that you're in command now."

"Only until Lee returns." The old man smiled. "A token promotion I assure you. Why do you mention it?"

"Can't you guess?" The doctor shrugged. "You know my position. Lee thinks that I sabotaged the beam control and I'm as good as under arrest. I want to clear myself."

"How?"

"There was a dead man lying beside the equipment. I want permission to examine the corpse."

"But why? The man is dead you know that, and you know also how and when he died. What good would it do to examine him again?"

"Maybe none, but—" The doctor sat for a while smoking and frowning as if trying to collect his thoughts and fit them with words.

"Look Carl. You were responsible for that machine in there. Right?"

"Yes."

"And now that it's broken down you're going to examine it. Right?"

"Of course, but what has that to do—"

"Please, Carl." The doctor gestured with the cigarette between his fingers. "You're going to strip it down and check each part. You're going to test it and find out just why it acted as it did." He stared at the old man. "You are going to do that, aren't you?"

"Naturally, that is what I must do, but I still can't see what you are driving at."

"Can't you?" The doctor smiled. "All I want is to do exactly the same as you propose doing. Only instead of taking a machine to pieces to find out why it stopped working, I want to take a corpse to pieces to find out why it moved."

"Are you serious?" Carl stared his amazement. "You know how that dead man was moved, the only way he could have been. Someone lifted him and placed him beside the machine."

"So Lee thinks. So everyone thinks, but I know better." Smoke coiled between the two men as the medico leaned forward. "Look, Carl. I'm not a fool and I don't happen to be a liar. I was on duty here in this room for several hours prior to the machine breaking down. I was here during the entire period from Lee checking the control until his return when Dennison began to scream. No one, and I mean no one, entered that ward other than me."

"Someone must have done. The body—"

"That's what condemns me," snapped the doctor. "They look at the body and they look at me and I can read their minds like a book. The body was moved. Therefore someone moved it. Therefore I'm lying when I state that no one entered the room. Therefore I'm the man who moved the body. But I didn't, Carl! I swear it!"

"I believe you," said the old man quietly. "But the body was moved. How do you account for that?"

"I can't." Irritably the medico crushed out his cigarette and lit another. "Look, I've been over this a thousand times, and it still doesn't make sense. I was in this room. I heard Dennison scream and before I could enter the ward Lee had joined me. Before either of us could enter a couple of my boys ran past with hypos. Then, while we were watching the dead man, Lee sent them to cremate the two bodies lying in the room between the ward and the one housing the beam control. Both of them went into the room, found one of the bodies missing, and reported back. Lee found the dead man lying beside the machine." He stared at the old man. "What do you make of that?"

"If you didn't move the body then the two assistants did."

"No. They weren't gone for very long, we could hear their footsteps, and even if one of them had wanted to do such crazy thing, he would have had to trust the other to keep quiet about it." He shrugged. "A case could be made out against the pair of them, I suppose, but how were they to know that Lee would order them into the other room, and how could they be certain that Dennison would scream at the right time?"

"They couldn't," admitted the old man slowly. He looked at the doctor. "You've got a theory?"

"A ghost of one, but there's still one thing I want to know. It could clear me perhaps, and then again it couldn't, but as commander you could request the information."

"What?"

"At what time did the beam control cease working? If it happened after Dennison died then I'm in the clear. I couldn't have touched the machine unobserved." He looked hopefully at the old man. "Do you know?"

"Yes, but it won't do you any good. The analytical banks have nothing to do with the actual carrier beam. Lee ordered that cut after I found the control inoperative." He shook his head. "I'm sorry, but the machine could have been tampered with at any time within several hours. I think that it was recent, we should have noticed something wrong otherwise, but I'm afraid that it doesn't help you."

CHAPTER 8

He groaned, twisting a little, and as memory returned opened his eyes and stared up at the curved metal of the hull. For a while he stared at it, letting life return to his numbed body, reliving again the horrible sensation of bouncing fall, the screams and shrieks and clamour of tearing metal and dislodged equipment. Wetness covered his face, a warm, sticky wetness, and touching his mouth he stared at fingers stained with blood.

"Jack!" The whisper was heavy with pain. "Jack. Help me."

"Seth!" Grimly the captain dragged himself to his feet, his lungs labouring in the thin air, and his teeth chattering with cold. "Where are you?"

"Here, beneath the control panel." The astrogator sucked in his breath as if with savage pain. "The chair supports snapped and I'm jammed in."

"I'll get you out." Grimly Jack struggled across the tilted floor of the control room, tides of blackness threatening to roar over his dimming consciousness and plunge him into a great pit of oblivion. He fought against it, biting his lips and gritting his teeth against the reviving pain.

"I've been awake for a long time," babbled the thin astrogator. "I called and called but you didn't answer." He grunted as Jack heaved at the twisted metal supports of the crumpled chair. "Steady."

"Are you hurt?"

"I'm not sure." Seth rubbed his leg and winced. "I should be. That damn chair almost cut me in two and I've lost the circulation in this leg." He coughed and doubled in sudden pain.

"What's the matter?"

"My ribs. I thought that I'd got off lucky. It feels like a couple of them are broken."

"Can you stand?" Jack swayed a little and grabbed at the edge of the control panel. "Try and make it, I'm all in."

"I'll make it," said the astrogator grimly. He breathed with shallow caution and slumped against the panel, staring in the dim emergency lighting at the blood-streaked face of the young captain. "What a crash. It's lucky that we're still alive."

"For how long?" Jack shook his head and fumbled at a cabinet. "Listen. Can you hear anything?"

"No, I—" Seth's pale features turned even whiter. "The air! It's escaping! Jack, we've got a leak!"

"I know." Phials clinked as the young man turned from the medical cabinet, a hypodermic in his hand. "Here, let me give you a nerve block against the pain. I'll have one too and then we can do something about the puncture."

Clumsily he drove the slender needle into the arm of the astrogator and pressed down on the plunger. Seth grunted as the contents of the syringe entered his vein, then with incredible suddenness straightened and took a deep breath.

"That's better. Now I can stand and take a decent breath." He reached for the syringe, and refilling it with a scintillating blue fluid, emptied it into the captain's arm.

"Take it easy," warned Jack seriously. "That nerve block hasn't done anything but paralyse the sensory nerves so that they can't carry pain messages from your injuries to your brain. You're still injured though, and if you breathe too deeply with those broken ribs you may puncture a lung."

"If I don't then we'll all die of air-lack." Seth stared at the wrecked control room. "What a mess. What shall we do, Jack, get in suits?"

"Not worth it. The hole must be small or all the air would have escaped by now. Release some trace-powder and we'll slap on a patch."

The thin man nodded, and taking a sealed container from a wall rack ripped off the seal. A fine powder plumed from the container, colourful and mist-like, drifting in the air like smoke, wavering as it followed the passage of escaping air. Seth followed it, a self-seal patch in hand, moving awkwardly through the wrecked vessel as he tracked the writhing mist. It plumed against the hull down towards the engine room, coating the metal with a brilliant patch, and he stared at it, examining the split in the inner hull before ripping the cover from the patch and pressing it firmly over the area.

The faint, almost ghost-like hissing ceased and he grinned as he struggled back to the control room.

Jack nodded to him as he entered, busy with a medical kit as he taped his broken nose and sprayed a clear plastic dressing over his skull.

"Fix it?"

"Yeah." Seth looked at the medical kit. "Shouldn't we examine the ship before treating ourselves?"

"We can do a better job after we've had some attention." He gestured towards the thin man. "Let me look at those ribs."

He frowned as he examined the broad, mottled streaks of bruise against the rib cage, then reached for a wide roll of elastic bandage and wrapped it tight around the other man's torso.

"You can expect some pain when the nerve block wears off. Don't make any sudden moves and try not to bend too much. Take shallow breaths and don't lift anything heavy. Those ribs are badly splintered and if they slash a lung you'll die of internal bleeding."

"I'll watch it," promised the astrogator. He shivered. "Space! It's cold in here."

"I've turned on the heaters and opened the spare air tanks." Jack nodded as he finished the dressing. "There, don't forget what I told you."

"Going to examine the ship now?"

"No. First we look at the others, if any are still alive, and then we'll have something hot to drive out this chill." He shrugged as he stared at the tilted control room. "The ship's a wreck anyway, that's obvious, and what's left of it can wait, but the men can't."

He was wrong.

The men could wait, wait for all eternity if they had to; wait with the calm, placid patience of the dead. Jack swallowed as he stared at them, their faces still twisted in the emotions they had experienced as they died. Fifteen of them, all dead, all stiffening as they lay, their blood staining the metal which had caused their death.

Some had died immediately, their bodies crushed when their harness had snapped and flung them with brutal force against the unyielding hull. Others had died more slowly, lying trapped with broken bodies, gasping and helpless in the dim-lit darkness, listening to the whine of escaping air.

Jack shuddered as he stared at their tormented faces.

Seth had food ready when he returned to the control room, cone-shaped thermocans salvaged from the ruined galley, and he passed one to the captain, thrusting in its top with his thumb. Jack took it, rolling it between his palms as he waited for the built-in chemical unit to heat the vitaminised soup.

"So they're all dead." Seth sipped at his own container. "We were lucky."

"The chairs saved us," said Jack quietly. "If it hadn't been for them—" He shuddered and gulped at the hot soup, trying to drive some of the chill from his shivering body and numbed brain. "What happened?"

"You forgot the orbital velocity, or maybe you just didn't have time to think about it." Seth lifted his thermocan. "I tried to warn you, but that damn mountain came along at the wrong time."

"Orbital velocity." Jack smiled, a bitter twisting of his lips, and stared sombrely at his steaming container. "A fine pilot I turned out to be. I stopped the ship all right, halted it relative to space, and then forgot that Mercury travels through the void at almost thirty miles a second. We'd stopped all right, but the planet hadn't, and with no atmosphere to transmit the motion we just hung there and let the planet come up and smack us down."

"You couldn't help it, Jack." Seth glowered at the humped bulk of the beam control. "If that contraption had worked this wouldn't have happened. If we hadn't had it at all we'd have been all right. It was relying on the damned thing that wrecked us. By the time you'd got the feel of the ship it was too late to do anything to avoid the crash. Now look at us: in a tin can somewhere on the night side, and we don't even know which way to head to get to the Station."

"We can find it," said Jack slowly. "We can take star sights and any way from the centre will lead to the Twilight Belt."

"The Belt stretches right around the planet," reminded the astrogator. "There's nine thousand miles of it."

"I know that, but it isn't as bad as it might be. I caught a glimpse of the dayside just before we crashed, and we must be nearer to the Belt than we think. The beam control had us guided towards the Station, so we can't be too far from it."

"Far enough. We can't walk all that way and we can't fly."

"There are some crawlers down in the hold; we could cut the hull and get one out. If we powered it from the ship's accumulators and stocked it with air and supplies we might be able to make it." Jack stared at the astrogator. "How do you feel about it?"

"Rotten." Seth finished his soup and threw the empty container against the hull. "We're on the night side of Mercury, don't forget. The region that not even the Station with all their equipment and men have not explored. How can a couple of half-crippled spacemen and a doubtful crawler do what your brother hasn't yet done? No, I don't think we'll try that, not until we have to, anyway."

"Maybe you're right." Jack reached for a fresh thermocan and thrust in the top. "If I know Lee he will have sent a party out for us as soon as he knew we were going to crash. The best thing we can do is to rig up some sort of a signal, a radio beacon or something like that." He stared at the shattered control panel. "If our transmitter works we could do it."

"What about the antenna? We'll have to get it pretty high if it's going to do any good."

"We rolled down a mountain didn't we?" Jack felt the dried blood crack on his face as he smiled. "Well? We can run a cable up the slope and mount the antenna on the summit. All we need is a repetitive signal, almost anything will do as long as it's broadcasting on the regular wavelength. If Lee has sent out a search party, and it's certain that he has, the crawlers will pick up the signal and head towards it."

"Sounds good." Seth frowned at the shattered panel. "When do we start?"

"As soon as we can rig up a transmitter. You look after that end and I'll sort out cable and something for an antenna." He grinned. "This should be easy."

Seth grunted, he didn't seem too optimistic.

And he was right.

Jack knew it as soon as they had left the ship, bulky and awkward in their regulation space suits, and he shivered and turned up the heating control.

"Jack?" The astrogator's voice came thinly over the inter-suit radio. "Can you hear me?"

"This isn't going to be easy. I'm losing heat fast and we haven't started yet."

"It must be due to conduction," said the young captain thoughtfully. "Normally we can only lose heat while in space by radiation, and we produce enough to counteract that in body heat alone. But now we're in contact with something cold, too cold, and it's draining the heat from our suits." He shivered. "Let's make a start anyway."

The ship lay like a crumpled tin can against a towering wall of what looked like ice, but it wasn't frozen water. It was frozen carbon dioxide, dry ice, and staring at it Jack knew why he'd had to keep the internal heaters on full blast to maintain the inside temperature. From the ship, sweeping up in a steep rampart, the side of the mountain down which they had rolled reared towards the coldly burning stars. It was rock, glittering with frozen gases and crystallised metals, and as they slipped and skidded on the patches of treacherous ice they felt the numbing of incredible cold slow their blood and numb their limbs.

"Jack, I can't stand much more of this." The astrogator's voice echoed his pain as he gasped into the radio. "I feel as if I were naked at the North Pole. We'll have to think of something else."

"Get back to the ship," ordered the captain. "I've got an idea."

He explained it as they warmed themselves at the glowing coils of an improvised heater.

"We'll wear double suits, rig the outer one up some way to fit, and lace between them with heater wires. We've enough charged Diracs to supply all the power we can use, and if we can get part way up the mountain it will help." He stared at the astrogator. "Ready?"

Seth nodded.

The next time they ventured outside the cold didn't seem quite so bad. The double suits with the laced wires of the heating elements enabled them to climb well above the gully, and Jack planted the radio antenna in a crack between two patches of ice. Then, paying out the cable as they went, they returned to the comfort of the ship.

"We'll try again," he decided. "I'm not satisfied with the position of the antenna. I'd like it to be higher, much higher. Every foot we can lift it will radiate the signal just that much further, don't forget."

"I'm not forgetting," muttered the astrogator. He held his hands close to the heater. "If only we didn't lose heat so fast." He stared at the captain. "We're fools! We're carrying armour in the hold, supplies for the Station, why the hell didn't we think of that before?"

"You're right!" Jack shook his head. "I don't know what's the matter with me. Let's break them out."

The next time they ventured from the ship they wore the heavy, glistening armour designed for the Station personnel. Slowly they struggled up the slippery mountainside, helping each other and trying not to touch the frozen surface more than was strictly necessary. Even at that, and with the heaters on at full power, they were shivering by the time they had doubled the antenna distance from the ship.

"Think that we'd better leave it at this, Jack?" The astrogator's teeth chattered as he spoke into the radio. "We've got to get back don't forget."

"A little further." The captain pointed with his armoured hand to where an outcrop glistened in the starlight. "We'll get it up there."

Grimly they lurched forward towards the high point.

It wasn't until they had fixed the antenna and had started back that they saw the creatures.

Black they were, midnight black, ovoid and featureless. They lay like patches of shadow on the downward path, and the area around the ship was ringed with them. Seth paused, almost touching one with his boot, and his voice echoed from the receiver.

"Think that they're dangerous, Jack?"

"How can they be?" The captain touched one with his boot. "They—"

He swore, throwing himself desperately back and away from the thing in his path, feeling himself fall as he tried to move his trapped foot, and rock smashed against his armour sending ugly sounds vibrating through his suit.

"Seth! Help me. It's got my foot!"

Frantically he lashed at the thing with his free boot, feeling the numb impact of his sole against something that felt like adamantine rock, and slowly, moving like some terrible leech, the black thing wrapped itself around his boot and began to creep up his leg.

Seth came then, kicking and jumping, slashing with a shard of stone and yelling insane curses in the hollow confines of his helmet.

He was wasting his time.

He could have been battering a boulder for all the impression he made, striking a river to make it stop flowing and, within the suit, Jack felt a terrible cold begin to sap his energy.

Desperately he clawed at his belt, tore a small Dirac from its connections adjusted the setting with trembling hands and flung the small accumulator from him as electrical energy flamed between the terminals.

The thing sensed it.

It hesitated in its upward progress, seemed almost to quiver then with agonising slowness it flowed away from the suit and towards the arcing flame of the Dirac.

Jack gulped and struggled to his feet.

"Quick, Seth, before others come."

"What was it? What did you do?" Panic thinned the echoing voice to a fine edge, and Jack gripped the suited man by the arm as they ran towards the safety of the ship.

"They're alive, some form of protoplasm, or maybe something else and they want heat and energy." Cautiously he threaded a path between more of the advancing horrors. "Heat attracts them, and we're radiating heat. When it grabbed my foot it began absorbing energy, and when I shorted the Dirac it decided that it would be better for it to shift to the greater energy source." He shuddered. "Look at them! All around the ship, drawn by the heat we're losing from the hull. Maybe they live on it, or need it for reproduction or something."

"Never mind that," said Seth grimly. "Unless we reach the ship soon we'll be shut out. Those damn leeches are crawling all over the hull."

It was true. A black tide had covered the area around the vessel, almost invisible in the starlight, and so black and light absorbing that they seemed but shadows. More appeared even as they watched, seeming to ooze from the very ground, and the gleaming metal of the battered hull was almost hidden by a swarm of flowing black shapes.

"Jack!" Sharp panic lifted the astrogator's voice to the thin edge of hysteria. "Look at those things! They'll be over the airlock soon."

"Yes." Jack forced his numbed legs to move even faster. "Hurry!"

"My God!" Seth echoed his horror over the radio. "Unless we get into the ship we'll die out here, and if those things cover the airlock—"

Desperately they raced over the frozen ground.

CHAPTER 9

They moved like glistening, squat-bodied insects through a hell of utter desolation, creeping with whining engines over jagged rock and skirting gaping chasms, hesitating as they climbed slippery masses of frozen gas, slewing and skidding as they crawled over the bleak, airless, frigid contortions of the mysterious night side.

Lee sat in the observation seat and stared grimly through the vision port.

"This is bad." Weston thinned his lips as he gripped the steering levers. "I've never been so deep before, and it's getting worse all the time." He glanced at the grim-faced commander. "Think we should try a different route?"

"No." Lee twisted in his seat and jerked his head at Blain. "Radio the others and have them come up to join us."

"Yes sir." The radio operator muttered into his instruments and Weston halted the vehicle with a falling hum from the powerful electric motors.

"I'll wait until we unite. This is no territory to cross alone."

Lee nodded, hating to admit the truth of what the captain said, and yet finding it impossible to deny. At first the going had been easy, the grey plain of the Twilight Belt slowly merging at the edge of the libration area into the jagged desolation of the night side. He had left one of the crawlers there, perched on a high outcrop of rock, waiting with its extended antenna for any messages to be relayed to the distant Station.

A second vehicle had been left further on, again perched as high as possible, the slender whip of the radio antenna just high enough for it to keep in contact with the base crawler. The other three had then plunged into the unknown, passing the known limits of exploration, driving deep into the frozen hell of the night side, feeling their way by the cold light of the burning stars and the beamless glare from their own searchlights.

But progress was slow.

Lee thought about it as he waited for the other two crawlers to follow their guide tracks and join the lead vehicle. Somewhere ahead of them the wrecked vessel waited, the essential component in its hold, lost amid the tangle of splintered rocks and glistening ice. Men might be there too, injured perhaps, helpless to do anything but wait for rescue. Lee swallowed as he imagined his brother, trapped perhaps, dying, staring with hopeless eyes towards the star-lit horizon, waiting for the rescue he must know would be coming.

And which, perhaps, would arrive too late.

Light sparkled from the crystalline surface of the surrounding plain, harsh, shadowless light glaring from the powerful searchlights of the other vehicles as they drew alongside.

"Contact the captains and ask them to come aboard," ordered Lee tiredly. He stared at Weston. "We can't carry on like this, progress is too slow, and there must be a better and faster way."

"There is. We—"

"Save it for when the others are here," interrupted Lee emotionlessly. "Blain, you had better get some food ready. No sense in wasting more time than we have to and we can eat as we talk."

The officer nodded, switching on the compact heat range and setting coffee to boil. He hesitated as he stared at the row of emergency thermocans, then shook his head as he powdered concentrated soup bricks into water. The thermocans, while easy and handy to use, were too expensive for normal use and had to be saved for strict emergencies. He sniffed at the steaming pot and added salt and powdered vitamins.

The other captains arrived just as the meal was ready.

They entered the crawler one after the other, huge in their armour, and grunted with relief as the heavy fabric and metal released their limbs.

"Smells good." Hughes smiled, and his companion, a short, scarred-faced man, grinned as he sat at the folding table.

"Nice work, Lee. We could all do with this." He glanced at the young commander. "Why the conference?"

"We've got a problem, Lacey. What would you say our speed has been recently?"

"Mile an hour. Actual distance covered towards objective, I mean. Why?"

"As far as Observation could figure out the ship crashed about a thousand miles from the Station. The first five hundred were easy, the plain had been levelled by alternation with heat and cold during the libration, and the next hundred weren't too bad, you'd all explored that region and knew the paths. But we've still a long way to go and at a mile an hour it's going to take too long."

"I've a suggestion," said Weston. "Why not send out advance parties? They can plot a route and save us all the backtracking we've had to do."

"That isn't going to help things much," said Hughes slowly. "The total speed wouldn't be much greater. Don't forget that an armoured man can't move very fast over this rock, and his range of vision wouldn't be much greater than it is from the cabins." He stared at Lee. "What do you think?"

"I'm not sure," said the young commander. "That's why I called you aboard, I want the benefit of your experience."

"Fair enough," said Lacey, his mouth full of bread and soup. "But it's the old problem. Unless you can get up really high these damn gullies defeat direct observation. If the night side were as flat as the day side it would be easy, but the crawlers can't travel like the shells, and in this light we've got to feel every inch of the way."

"Then you don't think it possible to increase our speed?"

"Not while we're passing through unexplored country. For one thing the crawlers can't fly, and if we get trapped in a blind gully we'll have to backtrack and try again. We might do that a dozen times, travel a hundred miles, and still have to come back to the point we started from." Lacey wiped his mouth and reached for a cigarette. "We're in a maze, a twisting collection of chasms, some of them filled with frozen gas, and if we're not careful the crawlers will drop into one and get buried." He shuddered. "That's something I don't even like thinking about."

"We can stay on the high ground," said Weston, "but Lacey's right. Night-side travel isn't easy at the best of times. Especially now when we're literally heading into the great unknown. Anything could lie before us, a chasm a mile deep, and stretching across the entire planet. A range of mountains without a break and with sheer walls. A pit of frozen gas without a solid bottom. Anything."

"Are you trying to tell me that I'm wasting my time trying to reach the wrecked vessel?" Lee stared coldly at the assembled captains and read his answer in their averted eyes and expressionless features. "Thank you, gentlemen, I can see that you do." His hand slammed against the frail table with an abrupt explosion of seething anger.

"What's the matter with you all? Don't you realise that your very attitude is dooming this expedition to failure without giving it a chance to succeed? I have sat here and listened to all your reasons just why we can't increase our progress. Gullies, you say, mountains, pits of frozen gas." He laughed with bitter curtness. "I wonder that you didn't mention ghosts and goblins at the same time."

"Be fair, Lee," urged Weston. "You can't ignore the facts."

"I'm not ignoring them, but accepting them doesn't mean that I must admit to defeat." He glared at the assembled captains. "Did men admit defeat when they stared up at the Moon and realised that it was a quarter of a million miles away? Did they sit down and shrug their shoulders when starvation threatened Earth after the Great Blight? Did we admit defeat when we built the Station and conquered the Twilight Belt? No, gentlemen. Obstacles are made to be overcome, and by Space we're going to reach that ship if we have to crawl there on hands and knees!"

"How?" said Lacey, and blew a thin streamer of smoke towards the instrument panel. "I've yet to see mere words lift a crawler over a mountain or keep it from falling into a chasm." The sneer in his voice reflected his inner contempt. Lee flushed.

"The only suggestion which has been made here is that men should act as a guide party. Weston made it and Hughes put his finger on why it wouldn't work as stated." He stared at his own captain. "But Weston had the right idea. While we remain cooped up in the crawlers we've got to fumble our way along."

"Of course." Lacey shrugged. "Even if men went ahead there's nothing to show them which way to go."

"But I know how it can be done." Lee pushed away the untasted food. "Listen. We take three men, one from each crawler. They can remain in radio contact and they will climb to the highest peak they can find. The crawlers will fire their cannon and illuminate the area. The men can then spot the most likely route and radio-direct the lead crawler to follow us. The last crawler will pick up the men until we reach the new high point and we'll repeat the manoeuvre." He stared at the captains. "Any questions?"

"Use one man," said Lacey abruptly. "Take him from the last vehicle and put three extra men on the first crawler. The lead machine can drop them off and the last crawler pick them up. We can travel faster that way without losing more time than necessary."

"Better make it two men," suggested Weston. "Those slopes are hard to climb and one man might get into serious trouble."

"We'll work it this way then. Two men from the rear crawler and they can be picked up after they have plotted the route. The second two from the centre machine and the final two from the lead vehicle. That way we can avoid all false tracks and will have to halt together only after covering as much distance as possible. Naturally the captains will remain with their crawlers." He stared at Lacey. "You will take the lead, it will save transferring your men to this vehicle, and Blain and I will make the first observation." He jerked his head towards the radio officer. "Get into your armour, Blain, we're wasting time."

The man nodded, and together they donned the stiff fabric and metal of the protective suiting.

The climb was a hard, long struggle, with booted feet slipping on icy rock, and gloved hands growing numb as they clawed their way towards the summit of the rearing outcrop beneath which the vehicles rested. Lee grunted as he reached the top and spoke quietly into his radio.

"Right. Fire a flare cannon. Forward and at about sixty degrees."

He squinted as the cannon belched fire and a scintillating incandescent projectile lanced from the squat muzzle and streamed upwards to the glistening stars. Light glowed from the eye-searing brilliance of burning magnesium, and as it rose the projectile bathed the entire area in a ghostly white illumination. High it rose, then expanded with the puff of a soundless explosion, and a fine shower of particles sprayed from the central point, each glowing with fierce brilliance as they spread across the heavens, falling swiftly through the airless void as the weak gravity of the planet drew them back.

Lee spoke quickly into his microphone.

"A gully leads off at a ten-degree angle about half a mile on. It tracks directly towards a cross chasm, but there seems to be a natural bridge to the left. From there drive at fifteen degrees until you reach the foothills of a mountain range. Bear right and unload your observers."

"Right." Lee could hear the whine of gears as Lacey fed power to his engines. Far below the squat shape of the crawler jerked as the wide treads clawed at the frozen soil, and even before it had begun to move the two men were slipping down the outcrop and towards the waiting vehicle. Barely had they passed through the airlock when it started with a jerk of treads, following the luminescent trail-powder dropped by the guide crawler.

Lee grinned as he swayed to the jolting of the speeding vehicle.

At the next observation point they passed the crawler waiting for its two men, and Weston chuckled as he fed power to the spinning wheels.

"Man! This is what I call travelling!"

"Let's hope that it lasts," said Lee hopefully. "If we carry on like this we should reach the ship in a few days. We can return the same way, too, the guide-powder will show us the way."

Blain said nothing, but sat smoking and staring through the vision ports, his thin face blank with thought.

They passed Lacey's crawler and took the lead, and again Lee and the radio man donned their suits and crawled painfully up the side of a jagged monstrosity of rock and squinted at the jumbled terrain in the brilliant glare of a flare projectile. This time Blain slipped when descending, rolling in a fury of threshing limbs and abruptly vanishing into a deep pit of frozen oxygen. Lee knelt at the side of the pit and heard the harsh breathing of the other man echo in his helmet.

"Blain! Are you all right?"

"Broke a leg, I think." Lee heard the sharp hiss of indrawn breath. "I can't move, this damned snow, and I'm losing heat fast."

"I'll get you out." Lee thrust his arm deep into the snow, lying on his face and extending his limb as far as possible. He touched something, rapped it, and heard Blain's voice.

"Is that you, Lee? Something's tapping against my helmet."

"Good. Lift up your arm and I'll pull you out."

He shivered as he gripped the armoured hands, and bracing himself dragged the limp figure half out of the snow-filled pit. Blain whimpered and the young commander sweated with effort as he lugged the heavy figure away from the treacherous hole.

"Blain! You're free now. Can you walk?"

"I don't know." The radio man's teeth chattered as he forced words through his numbed lips. "I can't move, Lee. I'm frozen or something. My leg—"

"Try." Lee hauled at the armoured figure. "Stand up, damn you! Stand up and hang on me. You want to die out here?"

The lash of his voice drove some of the numbness from the other man's chilled brain, and he scrabbled at the rock, twisting as he tried to get to his feet, then collapsed with a groan.

"It's no good, Lee. My leg's busted, I can feel it, the broken bone's ripping into my flesh."

"Hell!" Lee gritted his teeth and, stooping, heaved at the ungainly figure. He swayed, almost fell, then driving his body to the utmost he heaved the dead weight of man and armour on to his shoulders.

Cautiously he half walked, half slipped down the slope towards the waiting vehicle.

Weston helped him, lunging forward from the driving seat as Lee passed through the airlock, and tugging at the great globe of Blain's helmet. Lee unsealed his armour and pointed towards the controls.

"Get this thing moving, Weston. I'll attend to Blain."

"But—"

"You heard what I said. Now hurry!"

He stooped over the sick man as the crawler jerked into life and his hands were strangely gentle as he examined the unconscious figure. The leg was broken, probably in the fall and the jagged ends of the splintered bone protruded through the skin. Lee set it, splinting the limb and wrapping the wound with layers of plastic bandage. From a medical kit he took a hypodermic, and snapping the top from a phial of adrenaline injected the drug into the radio man's arm. Blain groaned and opened his eyes.

"How do you feel?"

"Rotten. My leg—" Blain bared his teeth in a grimace of pain.

"I'll give you a nerve block against that in a moment, but I want to know if you feel any other pain."

"No."

"Are you certain? No numbness? No dead feeling?"

"No."

"Good." Lee sighed with relief and reached for the scintillating blue fluid of the nerve block. "I was afraid that perhaps you'd got frozen. The temperature out there is down to almost the absolute and you were covered with a blanket of snow. The conduction alone must have almost drained your suit of heat." He hesitated, the hypodermic in his hand. "You're quite certain about that, Blain? Once I give you this you wouldn't feel it if you were shredded in a mincer."

"I'm certain." The radio man grinned. "You don't have to tell me to make sure. I've been out here before. Remember?"

"Sure." Lee smiled and injected the contents of the hypodermic into the great vein of the arm.

Weston looked up from the controls as he slumped in the companion seat.

"How is he?"

"Broken leg, but he'll be all right. How are we going?"

"Pretty good. The last observation showed a long stretch of fairly clear rock, looks almost like the edge of a planetary split to me, and we can follow it for miles." He looked at the young commander. "What happens now?"

"How do you mean?"

"Blain." Weston jerked his head. "You can't go out on observation alone."

"No," said Lee calmly. "You'll have to come with me, the crawler won't run away if it's left unattended."

"But what about the flare cannon? Who's going to fire that and take down your instructions?"

"Blain. I've given him a nerve block, but aside from a broken leg he's all right. He can do everything necessary but drive." Lee frowned as a muted hum came from the radio, the attention signal, and he threw a switch on the instrument panel.

"Lee here. What is it?"

"Lee?" Hughes's voice sounded thin and strained over the speaker. "I've just heard from Lacey. He's well below the horizon, this track we're following stretches for a hell of a way, luckily in the direction we want to follow."

"Well?" Lee tried to control his impatience. "What has Lacey to report?"

"He's run into trouble."

"What!"

"That's what he says. There's a barrier of some kind and he suggests we hold a conference."

"Conference, hell!" Lee scowled through the vision port. "Wait until we get up there and see what the trouble is. For all we know he may have hit anything, probably a pimple or a bit of broken ice." He broke the connection with a sweep of his palm and sat scowling at their illuminated path, impatient with the humming speed of the racing crawler.

He changed his opinion when they caught up with the halted vehicles.

Some planetary disturbance, probably eons old, when the invisible fingers of the sun's gravitational field had slowed the planet's rotation, had buckled the crust and thrown up a titanic wall of rock and frozen gases. Lee stared at it, tilting his head as he followed the barrier to the star-crowned ramparts.

"I thought that Lacey knew what he was talking about," said Weston quickly. "That's hardly a pimple."

"No." Lee stared at his captain. "So I apologise, now let's see how the hell to get over it." He flicked the switch of the radio. "Lacey? Hughes? Don suits and meet me outside."

He stared at Weston. "Back up a little and be ready to fire the flare cannon. I want to see just what it is we're up against."

"Right."

"We may be coming back in here, but it all depends." Fatigue marred the youthful lines of the commander's face. "Damn the luck! We were going so well. The ship can't be too far off now. If it hadn't been for that barrier—" He looked at Weston. "How are we for power?"

"Pretty good. Why?"

"I don't know. Just a thought. We've still got to get back and I don't want to lose any men." He shrugged. "Give me a hand with my suit, will you? I'm feeling all in."

Weston nodded and reached for the heavy armour.

CHAPTER 10

The barrier was titanic, and staring at it in the light of his head-beam, Lee felt the numbing constriction of despair. Beside him, monstrous in their armour, the other captains examined the great wall, and the sound of their voices murmured within the helmets.

"Basalt," said Hughes thoughtfully. "Probably thrown up when the planet finally yielded to the Solar drag."

"It's not all rock, though," pointed out Lacey. He stooped and prodded at the surface with a metal bar. "See? This stuff's dry ice."

"That's natural. Some of the gases would have been trapped and frozen. I wouldn't mind betting that most of this barrier is honeycombed with seams of ice and compressed snow. I've met similar formations before."

"Not as big as this, surely?"

"No." Hughes sighed. "It looks as if this is the end of line."

"What makes you think that?" Lee tried to keep his frustration from his voice. In imagination he saw the captain shrug.

"Isn't it obvious? The crawlers can't climb up that wall and, as far as we can tell, it runs for maybe a thousand miles across our path."

"It's the end all right," said Lacey, and there was a grim finality in his voice. "We'd need a jet scooter to get over that barrier."

"We haven't got a scooter, but I don't intend giving up now. For all we know the ship could be just beyond that barrier and I intend finding out." He tilted his helmet, staring up at the jagged wall of rock and ice. "Fire a charge, Weston. Let's see what's up there."

Behind him the flare cannon belched its load of scintillating flame, and in the brilliant light shadows crawled and writhed over the bleak surface.

"See!" Lee gestured with his arm. "About a hundred feet up. There's a ledge and what seems to be a split in the barrier." He strode forward in the dying light. "Let's see what's up there."

Painfully they clawed their way up the frigid barrier, climbing in the glare of the searchlights, their shadows huge and grotesque beneath the stars.

Later, in the warmth and comfort of the cabin, they talked over what they had found.

"The whole idea's fantastic," exploded Lacey. "I'll admit that perhaps we could get a crawler up that initial slope, and the ledge is wide enough to take it, but as for blasting a way through the barrier—" He shook his head. "Lee, you wouldn't stand a chance."

"Maybe not, but it's a chance and I want to take it." He stared at Hughes. "You admit that the barrier could be a honeycomb formation?"

"Yes, but—"

"I know what you're going to say," interrupted the young commander. "But this isn't Earth and there's no reason to suppose that the formation will be as thick as it would be back home. The gravity of Mercury is about the same as that on the Moon, and you know how thin some of the crater walls are."

"That's true, but you still don't know that the ship is beyond that barrier." Lacey scowled as he lit a cigarette. "I don't like this idea of risking all our necks for the sake of dead men."

"We can't be certain of that, Lacey."

"If they were still alive we would have heard them over the radio."

"Maybe their set was ruined, maybe anything." Lee shrugged. "Anyway, the crew isn't important, the cargo is, and you all know what that is."

"How do you propose to blast through?" Hughes sipped at his steaming coffee. "Even if this formation is no thicker than the Moon craters it's still going to be some job."

"We can do it," said Lee eagerly. "First we use the thermal units to melt the ice and solidified gases. The crawler can just about make it to the ledge, and once up there we can blast our way with the thermite bombs." He stared at Hughes, "You know a little more about such things than I. Can it be done?"

"Yes. The best way would be to drill a small hole deep into the compressed snow. Place a thermite charge and detonate it by remote control. The heat will cause the snow to expand back into gas and the pressure will be enormous. In this light gravity it will probably blast a great portion from the barrier, act as a high explosive and make a passage through the wall." He hesitated. "There'll be danger of flying particles, of course, and you'll have to pick a blast-path other than solid rock, but I'd say it could be done."

"The crawler will protect the crew from blast effect," said Lee. He stared at the assembled captains. "Naturally this will be a volunteer assignment. I shall go, and I think two other men will be more than enough. If you gentlemen will inform your crews?"

"Do that, Hughes," said Lacey. "Ask for one man." He grinned at the young commander through a cloud of smoke. "Count me in."

"And me," said Hughes.

"Wait a minute," snapped Weston. "What about me?"

"You'll have to stay behind, Weston." Lee smiled at the expression on the captain's face. "Someone must remain in command here, and we have a sick man to take care of." His voice took on the sharp note of command. "We'll use your crawler, Lacey. Take all the charges from the other two and rob them of what we need. First I suggest we blast a ramp to the ledge and make some preliminary blasts. That will give us an idea as to how deep we can go." He rose from the table. "If you're ready?"

The first stages were easy. One crawler remained close to the wall while the others retreated to a safe distance. Flame spat from the stubby thermal units mounted on the squat vehicle and snow puffed into a vanishing cloud as the unit sprayed the area with flaming thermite. Lee grunted as he examined the bared rock and gestured upwards.

Lacey climbed with him to the ledge and stood by, glistening in the light of the search beams as Lee rammed home the slim metal cylinders of the thermal charges.

"Right. You go down, Lacey. I'm going to climb a little higher and watch the effects of the blast."

"I'll stay with you," said the captain, and climbed slowly up the almost sheer wall of rock, his gloved hands clawing at the slippery stone. Lee hesitated then, shrugging, climbed after him, forcing his way upwards until the crawlers below looked tiny and small.

"Fire."

Something like smoke spouted from the mountain, jetting and expanding into a great vanishing cloud of ghostly shininess, the frozen oxygen converted to gas by the savage heat, and dissipating into the void. Rock quivered beneath the gloved hands of the watching men, then with deceptive slowness a great section of the wall seemed to billow, to crumple into a mass of jagged fragments and, with fresh spurts of released gas, sprayed from the mountain as if shot from the barrel of a mighty gun.

"Not bad," said Lacey calmly. "Let's see what happened."

It seemed incredible that so small a charge could have shifted so much rock, but staring at it Lee knew that it hadn't been so much the thermite itself as the forces it had released in the surrounding mass of time and cold weakened stone. The thermite had only served as a trigger, a form of detonator to the latent forces ready to expand with incredible fury against the surrounding barrier, aided to an incredible extent by the low gravitation.

"We'll set more charges by hand," he decided. "We'll have to enfilade anyway, otherwise the crawler will be damaged too much by falling rock." He strode forward as he spoke and began ramming fresh charges deep into the crevices among the rock, his head beam throwing a thousand glitters from mineral deposits and strange crystals. Lacey worked with him, both men moving with trained efficiency and this time made their way down the slope and into the crawler.

"Let her go!" Lee removed his helmet and squinted a little as he stared at the tremendous gout of shattered stone spewing from the barrier. Metallic clangs echoed through the cabin as debris fell against the outer hull, and Lacey flinched, then laughed as he realised the uselessness of his instinctive gesture.

"Let's get up there," he chuckled. "Now we're really beginning to move."

He swayed as the wide treads churned their cautious way up the debris-littered slope.

It became automatic after that. One after the other Lee and Lacey would plant the charges, ramming them far into the rock face with the help of a ram-bit driven by the crawler. Then they would enter the vehicle, the crawler would retreat to a niche blasted from the side wall, and the thermite would trigger the gases to rip another great section from the lengthening tunnel.

On Earth it would have been impossible. There the heavy atmosphere and the danger of blast waves would have combined with the gravity to smash the vehicle and bring down the roof of the crude tunnel. But there was no air on Mercury, the gravitation was light and the rock chilled to almost the absolute zero and as brittle as the thinnest glass.

Even so, passage was slow.

They lived in their heavy armour, their skin chaffed to angry soreness, and the bitter cold alternated with the warmth of the cabin mottled their faces with thin red lines, the traces of burst capillaries. Lacey suffered from frostbite and hobbled on a bandaged foot, while Hughes nursed bruised ribs, the result of not taking proper cover when firing a charge. It was after that near-tragic accident that Lee insisted that everyone enter the crawler before detonating the thermite.

Grimly they tunnelled their way through the tremendous mountain range.

Lee lost all track of time. He worked as they all did mechanically, moving stiffly and using the scintillating magic of the nerve block to erase the screaming agony of tormented flesh. They ate in snatches, sleeping when they were too tired to remain awake, falling log-like on the narrow bunks and forgetting the monotony of toil in brief oblivion.

He awoke to the impatient shaking of Lacey's hand

"Lee. Wake up."

"What?" The young commander yawned and rubbed his bristle-coated chin. "What's the matter?"

"We're almost out of thermite and the air is low."

"What!" Lee jerked awake and stared at the grim face of the captain. "Are you certain?"

"I don't make mistakes about a thing like that," said Lacey grimly. "I knew that you were too busy to keep an eye on things so I made it my business to check up." He hesitated. "We'll have to go back, Lee."

"No!" The young man strode towards the instrument panel and checked the gauges. "We can't go back now. For all we know another charge may see the end of the barrier."

"If we don't start back we may never live to see either side of the barrier," said Lacey curtly. "Be sensible, man. We can't breathe space."

"I know that," snapped Lee impatiently. "But there's another way." He flipped the switch of the radio. "Hello! Hello! Weston. Lee calling. Answer."

A low hum came from the instrument, the soft blurring of the carrier wave, but the speaker remained silent.

"Answer, damn you!" Lee almost snarled at the silent radio. "Weston! Lee calling. Come in."

"Is it broken?" Hughes stared at the silent radio. "They should have answered by now. Weston promised to maintain a continuous radio watch."

"It's not broken," snapped Lacey, and glared at the glistening tunnel, white in the glare of the searchlights. "I'll take a bet that this rock contains some deflecting mineral. We're just not getting through to Weston, the radio is nullified by the barrier."

"You're right." Lee closed his eyes and squeezed his thumb and forefinger against either side of his nose. "How much air have we, Lacey?"

"Just about enough to get back if we don't waste anymore the way we have been doing." The captain shrugged. "If you want to know about the thermite, then we've enough for a couple of more charges, and I'm counting everything, the thermal unit charges as well."

"We'll have to restock, Lee," said Hughes quietly. "Even if we broke through we still couldn't chance it."

"We can get air," snapped the young commander. "It's lying all around us." He smiled at their expressions. "The snow," he explained. "Most of it is frozen oxygen and we can bring it inside and thaw it out if we have to."

"Not while I'm still alive," gritted Lacey. "I knew a man who tried that once. Oh it worked all right, that is he thawed out something else at the same time. The stuff was mixed and he treated himself to a large dose of ammonia." He shrugged. "He didn't have time to try again, and he never lived to repeat the mistake. No, Lee. I know as well as you do that we're surrounded by useable gases, but it needs a laboratory to test them."

"He's right, Lee. That's the way we get our air for use at the Station and the vehicles. The night side crews spend most of their time collecting frozen gases."

"I know that," said Lee curtly. "Or are you forgetting that I'm the Station Commander?"

"No, Lee, I'm not forgetting."

"Sorry." Lee smiled at Hughes's flushed features. "I'm tired and worried sick about my brother." He frowned. "I don't want to backtrack in case the roof comes down. The vibration of the treads could start a fall that would bury us beneath tons of rock, smash us flatter than an air seal, and we'd never know what hit us. If someone could walk back?"

"You'd never make it, Lee," snapped Lacey. "I know what's in your mind, but even if you did get through, how are you going to bring us the air? On your back?"

"No." Lee sighed and his shoulders slumped as he stared through the vision ports. "That damn radio! Well, we may as well use the last of the thermite. Will you set them Lacey?"

"Sure."

Dully Lee watched as the armoured figure strode into the glare of the searchlights and tamped the slender thermite containers into a crack in the far wall. He frowned as the armoured figure paused and leaned towards the radio. "Lacey. Can you hear me?"

"Just about. Why?"

"Come on in. I want to fire the charges."

"Just a minute, I—" Lacey tugged at something imbedded in the shattered surface of the rock. Then, apparently giving up, he re-entered the crawler.

"What kept you?"

"Something imbedded in the wall, looked like an artifact to me, and if it is it's older than time itself."

Lee shrugged, not feeling any interest in something with which he normally would have felt keen excitement.

Impatiently he pressed the firing control, and before him, exploding in soundless fury, the mingled rock and ice billowed in splintered ruin. Gas plumed about them, expanding and dissipating beneath the savage heat of the thermite, and the hull rang and thundered to the impact of flying particles.

"That's the last," said Lacey grimly. "And if we don't hurry—" He paused, letting his words die into silence, and beside him Hughes muttered something which sounded like a cross between an oath and a prayer.

"We're through! Lee! We've done it!"

"Yes," said the young commander dully. "We've broken through the mountain—but what good does it do us?"

Sombrely he stared through the vision port at the jagged edge of the tunnel's end, and the coldly glistening stars revealed in all their naked glory, framed by a circle of shattered stone, seemed to stare with impassive mockery.

They had reached the end of the barrier—but they had no air!

CHAPTER II

It was cold in the ship, and the two men huddled over the glowing coils of the heater, little white plumes spilling from between their lips as they exhaled in the frigid air. Thermo-cans littered the floor around them, empty, lying where they had been flung, and Dirac accumulators almost hid the smooth metal of the tilted floor.

Jack stared at them, then at the thick cables snaking from them to the hull, and shifted uncomfortably on his insulated seat.

"Think we should give them another dose, Seth?"

"Not until we have to," said the astrogator grimly, and shuddered as he stared at the warped metal of the inner hull.

"Electric current drives them off when their weight threatens to crush the ship, but the damn things come back for more, and each time it takes more current to drive them off." He shuddered again. "How long will it be before they break in?"

"Maybe never." Jack shivered and reached for a fresh thermo-can. He lifted it, poising it between his palms, and looked at the astrogator. "How do we stand for food, Seth?"

"We could do with more, or maybe we've got too much, it depends on how you look at it."

"How long can we last if those leeches don't break in?"

"About a week. Maybe two if we don't eat for the last ten days." Seth cursed as he picked up a can. "To hell with it. Let's eat. May as well die in comfort." He thrust in the top of the cone-shaped can. "I wish your brother would hurry up. You certain that he'll come?"

"He'll come. We may be dead by the time he gets here, but I know Lee, and nothing will stop him."

"Nothing?" Seth sniffed at the steam rising from the container. "He's got a whole planet lined up against him, Jack, and no man can work miracles."

"Lee can."

"Then let's hope that his miracle-working talents are in full swing. Unless he gets here soon then he may as well save his breath and time."

"He'll get here. You forget what's in our cargo."

"That damned beam control." Seth cursed with savage intensity. "Let it rot. As far as I'm concerned if he arrives a second after I'm dead then he needn't arrive at all. Why should I worry about what happens after I kick off?"

"You don't mean that, Seth." Jack thrust in the top of his own can and, while waiting for it to heat, crossed the room to the shattered instrument panel. Carefully he examined the radio transmitter, then shook his head. "I don't get it. Either this thing isn't broadcasting or we're surrounded by something that stops the radio waves. Lee must have arrived in this area by now."

"You hope." Seth gulped his steaming soup and crossed to the control panel. "Anything on the visiscreen?"

"I doubt it." Jack snapped the rheostat and the surface of the view plate flickered, but remained dark. "Are you sure you repaired this, Seth?"

"Sure I'm sure, you saw me do it, and you know the trouble we had fixing a new 'eye'." The astrogator glowered at the dark surface. "It's those leeches. They're crawling all over the hull again and soaking up our radiated heat." His hand tightened on the thin metal of the container, gripping it until the can crumpled to ruin. Dully he stared at it, then with savage fury flung it into a corner.

"Damn it, Jack! How much longer must we stand this? Cooped up here waiting for those heat-leeches to smash the hull or freeze us to death. Little food and no radio, and no way of knowing if help is coming or not. Can't we do something about it?"

"What?"

"Fix up a crawler or something. With those thermal units and flare cannon maybe we could blast a way through the leeches. At least we could try. Anything would be better than just sitting here waiting for death."

"We can't fix a crawler and you know it. We tried, but the crash junked most of the parts and, anyway, we haven't the room to assemble one. The only thing we can do is to put on armour, load ourselves with thermite charges and try to bomb our way through." He shrugged. "Even at that I doubt if it would work. Those things love heat and radiation and there are thousands of them. We wouldn't stand a chance."

"I guess you're right," said the astrogator reluctantly. "But it's this waiting! I—" He paused, head tilted and mouth half open as though he had caught some sudden sound, and staring at him Jack felt a swift fear.

"What's the matter?"

"Listen!" Seth made a sharp gesture with his hand. "Can you hear it?"

"Yes, I—" Jack grabbed at the thin man. "Quick!"

Desperately they sprang towards the insulated chairs while around them grew a soft, peculiar, almost inaudible sound. It was a faint creaking, a rustling, an almost silent protestation from over-strained stanchions and yielding plates. Spaceships were designed to have tremendous strength along the fore and aft axis, strength essential to withstand the enormous thrust of the rocket drive, but otherwise they were relatively weak. With hulls subject to an internal pressure of no more than fifteen pounds, and designed with weight as the main consideration, they could withstand little external pressure sharp impacts, or unusual stresses. When the ship had crashed most of the outer hull had been stripped away and several of the bracing members twisted beyond usefulness. Now with the increasing weight of the strange leeches piling against and on the inner plates, the danger of being crushed was very near.

Jack waited until they had seated themselves in the insulated chairs, then leaning over threw a switch connected to the piled Dirac accumulators.

Power flowed from them, torrents of electrical energy streaming along the cables and into the hull of the ship Sparks crackled and snapped from every point, flaring and arcing, dulling the dim glow of the lights and filling the air with the reek of ozone.

"Give 'em some more," whispered Seth fearfully, and his eyes as he stared at the sagging plates of the inner hull held an almost frantic terror. "Quick, before they break in."

"I've given them all we've got," said Jack quietly. "I've hooked nearly all the Diracs we carried to the main circuit, and if that doesn't make them run nothing will."

Tensely they waited, their faces strained in the blue-shot lighting, and slowly, too slowly, the sagging of the plates ceased and the soft, almost inaudible murmur of complaining metal died into silence. Jack stretched out his hand towards the switch.

"Hold it, Jack." Seth nervously licked his lips, looking a little like a thin devil as he sat, hunched and doubled, his thin features limned by the flaring light of the electrical discharges. "Let the devils get well away. For all we know they may be barricading our radio signals. Anyway, I'll feel a lot better when I know that they've left the hull."

"It's wasting current," reminded the captain, but he didn't break the circuit. Like the astrogator he too felt the grim horror of the spaceman for crawling things and missed the clean, star-shot void. Suddenly he wanted to see the stars again. "I'll leave it on until they clear away from the visi-screen eye," he promised. "Maybe we can spot something then."

Seth shrugged, he didn't look too hopeful.

It took a long time for the leeches to clear away from the hull, and Jack stared grimly at the registration dials on the small accumulators as he broke the circuit. The terrible drain had almost exhausted the incredibly powerful batteries, and he knew that the next time they had to rely on them would be the last.

Slowly he joined the astrogator at the control panel, staring at the flickering surface of the repaired visiscreen and feeling a sudden nostalgia as he stared at the remote beauty of the distant stars.

"This place is like one of the Moon craters," said the astrogator as he adjusted the directional control. "See how the walls rise from the bottom? I'll bet that they are even steeper outside, they're bad enough here, but at least we can walk up them. Or we could if we didn't have those leeches to worry about."

"Perhaps this is a crater," suggested the captain. "I don't remember Lee ever telling me about the heat-leeches before, and if they were general they would surely be found close to the day side. The heat would be bound to attract them." He frowned. "If this is a tremendous crater it would account for it. The things may have a vein of radioactive ore near here and can't wander too far away from it. They would stay cooped up within those high walls." He stared at the towering ramparts. "Look at them! Miles high and covered with ice and frozen gases."

"A hell of a place to land," agreed Seth. He looked at the young captain. "If what you say is true, Jack, where does it put us?"

"How do you mean?"

"You know what I mean. If this," Seth gestured towards the screen, "is just an enormous crater like the ones on the Moon, then how the hell are we going to get out?"

"Lee—"

"I know all about that Lee, but that doesn't mean a thing." Seth pointed to the steep slope on which they had planted the radio antenna. "Look at it! No crawler could climb to the top of that mountain, and you say that the other side could be worse. If it is, and I reckon it must be, what chance have we got?"

"I don't know," said Jack slowly. "But I do know this. If there is a way Lee will find it. I—" He broke off, staring at the flickering surface of the plate, and when he spoke again incredulous excitement throbbed in his voice. "Seth! Look!"

"Where? What at?"

"There, you fool! About a quarter of the way up the slope. See it?"

"No."

"Try again. Sec?" Jack rested his finger on the screen, and Seth grunted. "Now I see it, looks like a cave or something." He sucked in his breath with a hissing exclamation.

"Jack! Look!" His voice sounded almost like a prayer. "Men!"

He was right.

Tiny they were against the vastness of the great slope, lit only by the stars and a soft radiance, which seemed to come from somewhere behind them, standing like little dolls at the edge of the newly-made opening. Watching them, Jack felt a surge of panic.

"We've got to signal to them in some way. Seth, try the radio again."

"Why?" The astrogator didn't seem able to tear his gaze away from the screen. "They'll find us. They can't miss the ship at this distance."

"I'm not taking any chances," snapped the young captain. "Don't forget those leeches are all around us, probably all over the hull as well. How can they tell that we're down here unless we signal?"

"What are you going to do?"

"Put on a suit and explode some thermite charges. That should attract their attention." Jack bit his lip as he stared at the visiscreen. "Keep trying to contact them by radio."

Seth nodded, his fingers working the improvised key, and Jack hastily donned one of the suits of armour. Stepping towards the airlock he made certain that the thermite charges in his belt were set for instant ignition, then stepping into the vestibule he closed the inner door and waited for the pumps to evacuate the compartment.

Slowly he opened the outer door.

Blackness ebbed around him, a surging tide of ebon-skinned leeches, heaving slightly as they made their slow way back towards the hull, eager to absorb the heat radiation of the wrecked vessel. Jack stared down at them for a moment, then, as if sensing his presence, they oozed towards him.

Desperately he tore the thermite bombs from his belt, pulled at the fuses, and threw them in a wide arc well away from the ship. They ignited, glowing with tremendous heat, and the leeches surged towards the streaming energy, then as if realising that the glowing masses of burning aluminium and iron oxide were dangerous recoiled from the spouting plumes of expanding gases.

Seth looked up from where he crouched over the transmitter, and his fingers moved with trained speed as he sent out the Interplanetary distress signal.

"Did they see you?"

"I don't know." Jack swung back his helmet and stared at the flickering visiscreen. "I hope so, the leeches are so thick that we'll have trouble getting out even if they do come." He grunted as brilliant light shone from the ragged edge of the hole. "Look! That's a crawler, see the lights?"

"Then why don't they answer?" Seth adjusted a control, his fingers never ceasing from working the key. "I've tried the whole waveband and—"

Sound crackled from the speaker, a shrill, peculiar hum, then, thin and faint, almost ghost-like against the background of blurring static, a man's voice echoed through the silent ship.

"Hello! Hello! Is that you, Jack?"

"Lee!" The young captain snatched at the microphone. "Thank heaven you've come. This is Jack speaking. Can you hear me?"

"Only just." The voice faded beneath a burst of static. "There's something peculiar about these mountains. They act as a radio barrier. If we hadn't seen your visual signal we'd never have guessed how near you were. How are you?"

"Rotten," snapped Seth impatiently. "Cut the talk and come and get us."

"That was Seth, the astrogator," explained Jack. "He's getting a little impatient."

"He won't have to wait much longer," said the fading voice. "We'll be back soon and—"

"Back!" Seth almost yelled into the microphone. "What the hell do you mean?"

"What I say!" Tired irritation sounded in the thin voice. "You can hang on until we get there, can't you?"

"Lee." Jack spoke quietly and glared at the thin astrogator. "How long will you be?"

"I don't know," confessed the young commander. "We had to tunnel through the mountain and now we're almost out of air. A couple of days perhaps. Maybe a little longer. Why?"

"We can't wait that long, Lee."

"Can't? Why not?"

"Can you see anything around the ship? Things like black leeches, big things, almost covering the hull?"

"Yes."

"They're alive, Lee. We've had to electrify the hull to drive them off and we have almost exhausted the power. We won't be alive in two days, Lee, none of us."

"I see." The radio fell silent, as if the men in the crawler were holding a conference. "Jack?"

"Here."

"Look, Jack, there's not much we can do. The air is low in the crawler, and anyway we haven't room for all of you. Can't you figure something out?"

"Won't the crawler hold a couple of extra men?"

"Yes, but—"

"All the rest are dead, Lee," said Jack quietly. "Seth and I are the only two who survived the crash. We have plenty of air left, more than enough to restock the crawler, and we could blast a way to you with the thermite charges." He gripped the handset until his knuckles shone white beneath the skin. "You've got to take us off, Lee. You've got to!"

"Yes." Again came the silence as men spoke and made plans. "What about the spare component for the beam control? Did that ride through the crash?"

"I think so. I checked the stores and the crate didn't seem to be damaged. Why?"

"I want it, Jack. That's why we are here—to get the spare component."

"To hell with the component!" yelled Seth. "What about us?"

"I'll save you as well if possible, but the beam control must come first." There was a grim reality in the commander's tone. "Now. As far as I can see we're about a mile from you up the slope. Can a crawler get down there and up again?"

"I should think so. The descent would be easy and you could climb it by tracking." Jack hesitated. "Don't forget those leeches I told you about. I almost got caught by one and was lucky to get away alive."

"Bad are they?"

"Very. Your heat will attract them, and there are enough of the things, to crush the hull. Be careful, Lee."

"I'll be careful," promised the commander grimly. "Now, here's what you do. Collect all the thermite charges you can and get the spare component ready by the airlock. I'm going to fire the flare-cannon, aim it low so that the burning magnesium will scatter over the foot of the slope and well away from the ship. If these leeches of yours do as I think they will, they will desert the hull for the heat of the flare charges. While they are busy wrap up a bundle of thermite and tie it on to the end of the line I'm going to shoot towards you. It's only thin wire, but it should do. Understand?"

"Yes, but—"

"No 'buts'." Lee chuckled. "We haven't any charges for the thermal units and I want some sort of protection before I drive down among those black devils. Ready now?"

"Ready."

Jack squinted as the squat muzzle of the flare-cannon lowered and blasted a rain of scintillating particles towards the swelling black sea of heat-leeches. Before the first burst had landed he was standing in the airlock, his helmet sealed and a great bundle of the slender thermite charges resting in the vestibule beside him. Tensely he waited for Seth to warn him when the path was clear.

"Ready?" The astrogator's voice echoed in the great helmet. "Those black devils are moving away towards the flare-cannon charges. Hell! I didn't think they could move so fast!"

"Normally they couldn't," explained Jack. "But they've been draining heat and energy from the ship for a long time now and it's probably speeded their metabolism. Have they fired the line yet?"

"Not yet." Seth hesitated. "I think—Yes! Here it comes now, Jack. Hurry!"

Quickly he opened the outer door, dragging the bundle after him and searching desperately for the thin wire. Once he stumbled, falling heavily to the frozen rock, and an ominous tide of oozing black halted its slow movement away from the hull and surged towards him.

"Jack! Hurry!"

"The line," he panted. "I can't find the line." He tripped again, stumbling as he tried to maintain his balance in the heavy armour, and, as he staggered, something caught across his foot, tripping him and throwing him hard against the warped metal of the hull. He stared down at it, narrowing his eyes in the glare of the reflected headbeam, and grabbed at something thin and black.

The line!

Rapidly he tied it to the bundle of thermite and yelled terse orders into the radio.

"Take it away! Quick!"

He jumped back as a round black nightmare oozed towards his foot, jumped painfully over a surging ribbon of coalesced bodies and dived for the safety of the airlock. Frantically he slammed the outer door, swinging the portal just as a leech crawled up the hull and towards the opening. Metal met something not quite flesh and not quite rock, a blend of alien chemistry and incredible life, and the door shuddered to a halt at Jack strained at it, prevented from closing by the ebon shape of an advancing leech.

"Jack!" Seth's voice sounded strained and cracked over the radio. "What's keeping you? Hurry!"

"The door's jammed," panted the young captain, and muscles knotted in his shoulders and arms as he strained a: the door. "I can't close it."

"You what!" Horror thinned the astrogator's voice. "Hold on, Jack. I'll put on a suit and open the inner door. Don't let the thing touch you."

Jack grunted, knowing that what the astrogator proposed was useless, for the inner door opened inward, and the man hadn't yet been born who could swing open that door with fifteen pounds pressing against every square inch of its inner surface. Over four tons, and no leverage. Before Seth could open the panel he would have to evacuate the ship, and that took time, too much time.

Grimly he stared at the black horror forcing its way into the vestibule, his broad shoulders straining against the door while his gloved hands searched frantically at his belt for a flare, a Dirac, anything which could serve as a weapon.

He touched a thermite charge.

Frantically he ripped it from his belt, tore at the fuse and flung it on the metal floor just in front of the oozing leech. Sparks flew as the charge ignited, then heat, tremendous heat seared from the burning compound. It spread, eating through the metal of the floor, melting the alloy as though it had been wax. Around it metal glowed with white heat, dulling to a sombre red, then to smoking black. It glowed with incandescent fury and Jack stepped back, shielding his eyes, his back pressed hard against the inner door.

The leech shuddered.

It twitched, seeming to attempt the impossible task of moving in two directions at once, its instinct driving it towards the source of heat and energy, and yet some dimly aware sense of danger trying to move it back. Instinct won and with a slithering, amoeba-like motion, it lurched, oozing over the scintillating fury on the floor, covering it with its strange, rock-like body.

Fire battled against alien flesh, and an organism designed to absorb the tiny amounts of energy to be found in a region of near absolute zero, tried to soak up the incredible heat of the burning compound. For a moment it seemed that the alien would do the impossible, and Jack stared at it, leaning heavily against the outer panel, feeling a sick helplessness as he watched the utter blackness of the sprawling leech.

Fire spurted from it, seeming to illuminate the gross body with inner flame, and it shuddered, heaved, and then, with shocking abruptness, collapsed, shrivelling and curling into a knotted heap of charred and shrunken tissue.

The thermite had won.

CHAPTER 12

Jack sighed with relief as he kicked the dried husk out of the vestibule and slammed the outer panel just in time to prevent more of the crawling horrors from entering the ship. Air whined as he spun the valves, escaping from the hole burned through the floor, and yet equalising the pressure enough for him to force open the door and stumble into the ship.

Seth looked up from where he stood, ready to open the air valves and evacuate the vessel.

"Jack! So you made it."

"Yes." The young captain swung back his helmet. "I had to ruin the airlock, and the next time we use it will be the last." He strode over to the visiscreen and stared at the distant glow of the crawler.

"Lee. Did you get the thermite?"

The radio crackled and voices, stronger than before, echoed through the control room.

"Yes."

"When are you coming for us?"

"Starting now." Lee sounded grim. "Better have plenty of air ready for us. We're living in armour and the suit tanks are getting low."

"Everything is ready and waiting. Air, thermite, the component and what food we have left."

"Never mind the food." A soft drone came from the radio, the sound of engines whining as they drove the crawler from the edge of the tunnel and on to the slope. "Here's what you do. As soon as we get near you open both doors of the airlock and divert the leeches with thermite charges. Lay them in a double row so that we can run between them. Lacey and I will leave the crawler and you'll pass the air and other stuff out to us. As soon as we're loaded we take off and drive back up the slope."

"I understand."

"You'd better," said Lee grimly. "There mustn't be any slips or delays. Stop, load and off. In that order, and I swear that I'll leave any man who messes up the schedule."

"You won't have to," said Jack. "We're as anxious to leave as you are."

"Right." The engine drone sounded louder. "Here we come!"

The radio clicked into silence, and on the flickering surface of the visiscreen a tiny mote, glaring with the multiple eyes of great searchlights, spouting scintillating glory from its squat flare-cannon, erupting masses of flaming thermite from its thermal units, came lunging down the steep, slippery mountainside.

Jack watched it, thinning his lips as he saw it slew, the wide treads spinning in the starlight and churning the ice-encrusted rock to gouged desolation. Nearer it came, nearer, while around it the black, amoeba-like heat-leeches shrivelled to withered husks as they tried to absorb the searing heat of the thermite, or crawled after the scattered heat spots spread by the flare-cannon.

"Get ready," he snapped to the thin astrogator. "Here they come."

Together they shut and sealed the great helmets, their breath whispering over the inter-suit radios, and around them, whining like a lost soul, the air rushed into space as they spun the release valves.

"Shall we open the doors now?" Seth swallowed, the sound coming clearly over the radio.

"Not yet. Open the inner door, but leave the outer one shut until they get here. You got your thermite ready?"

"Yes." Seth tripped the locks and swung wide the inner door of the airlock. "When you give word I'll swing into action." He swallowed again. "Space, but I hope that there's no slip up. We could never replace all that air."

"Lee won't let us down," said Jack quietly. "I told you that he'd send out for us, and he did. I knew that he'd find us, he's out there now. Quit worrying, Seth, you've nothing to worry about." He stiffened as his brother's voice rang from his receivers. "Right, Seth. Now!"

Smoothly they swung into action, the outer door opening on the bleak, frozen surface of the tiny world, and thermite charges flying from their hands to sear the assembled leeches at the base of the airlock. Frantically they scattered the scintillating charges, fighting the oozing tide of ebon shapes and, as they scattered the incendiary material the crawler lurched up to the gaping port.

"Quick!" Lee's voice reflected his inner tension. "Those damn things are learning. They're avoiding the thermite and heading for the crawler." He jumped from the vehicle as he spoke, the armoured figure of Lacey following, and with desperate haste Jack and the astrogator passed the slender tanks of liquid oxygen, the bundles of thermite and lastly, handling it with awkward care, the crated mass of the spare component.

It was heavy and clumsy, and the men sweated as they eased it through the open port and towards the narrow airlock of the crawler. Lee swore with savage violence and Lacey cursed as they tried to get the box through the too-narrow opening.

"It's too big, Lee. It won't go in."

"It's got to go in," gritted the commander. "It's got to." The light from his headbeam shone on the stencilled crate. "If we took it from the box?"

"No time." A desperate urgency tingled in Lacey's voice. "Those leeches, they're coming for us. Lee, let's get away from here!"

"No!"

"Damn the machine," snarled Seth, and the light from his helmet light shone on the black mass of the advancing leeches. "Leave it to rot."

"I came for this thing and by space I'm not going without it." Lee tore at the fastenings. "Hold them off with thermite while I unfasten this crate. Hurry!"

Around the crawler searing flame spurted from the flung thermite charges, and oozing, monstrous life shrivelled as they tried to absorb the radiant energy. Dozens died, crisped husks, their strange metabolism overloaded by the fierce heat, but more came on, more, and now they no longer flowed towards the too-savage sources of the energy on which they lived, but with alien caution advanced towards the crawler and the sweating men.

"For God's sake, Lee," pleaded Seth. "Let's get away from here."

"No."

"Unless we go soon, Lee," panted Lacey, "we won't be able to move at all." He swore as he flung more charges.

"A few more seconds—" Lee grunted as the last fastening came loose and tore at the covering of the assembled component. "Jack! Help me get this thing inside."

Carefully they lifted the machine, small enough now that it was free of its thick packing to slide through the port, and Hughes took the far end, grunting as he eased it to the floor.

"Right. Now let's get out of here. Seth! Jack! Lacey! Get inside. Hughes! Fire the thermal units and flare-cannon. Quick now!" Lee grabbed at the charges in his belt and flung a double handful of the searing incendiaries on the frozen ground at his feet. Quickly he lunged through the airlock and towards the driving seat, Hughes slamming the double doors behind him and Lacey spinning the valves on the air cylinders, replenishing the crawler with the vital oxygen.

Engines whined as Lee fed power to the coils, and the vehicle jerked as the wide treads clawed at the slick rock. It shuddered, seemed to fight against a hampering barrier, and the whining motors slowed as Lee jerked at the driving levers. Abruptly the pitch of the engines rose and the crawler lurched, slowed again, then shuddered as if ploughing through a sea of treacle.

"What's the matter?" Lacey stared red-eyed at the flickering needles on the instrument dials, his helmet swung back on his shoulders and his face red with the bitter chill inside the cabin.

"The leeches." Lee grunted as he swung back his own helmet, he other following his example. "They've piled up around the treads and the base of the crawler. We'll have to blast them free before we can move."

"Shall I go outside and scatter more thermite?" Jack began to seal his helmet, then swung it up at his brother's impatient gesture.

"No. If you try that they'll get you and we'll never be able to effect a rescue." He stared at the instrument panel. "Load the thermal units, fill the hoppers to the brim, we'll have to burn them away and trust to luck that we don't melt the tread."

Grimly he reached for the controls and again the crawler shuddered as the powerful engines fought to spin the treads against the massed bodies of the assembled leeches. Lee held down the power lever, waiting until the entire vehicle vibrated as though shaken by a mighty hand then, with a quick movement, flipped the switches of the thermal units

Heat sprayed from them, the searing heat of exploded thermite, spraying as the units scattered it around the vehicle. For a moment it seemed as if nothing had changed, as if the units, designed to rip away the surface ice and frozen gases of the night side, had failed. Then the engines rose in pitch, the vibrating ceased, and with a lurching shudder the crawler ground forward.

"Done it!" Sweat glistened on the commander's taut features. "Now if we can only keep moving—"

Silence fell in the crowded cabin, broken only by the whine of the engine and the transmitted sound of the treads as they spun over the driving wheels, clawing at the icy rock of the slope, forcing the overloaded vehicle towards the almost invisible point where the ragged edge of the tunnel gaped like a black shadow among shadows.

Behind them came the heat-leeches.

They were slow, but fed by relative torrents of unaccustomed energy their metabolism had speeded until they flowed almost as fast as the labouring crawler. Lee watched them, his eyes flickering from the fore vision ports to the rearward screen, and as he gauged their advance with their own progress deep lines of fatigue and worry aged his normally youthful features.

"Are we going to make it?" Lacey leaned forward, his sore eyes hot as they stared at the slowly moving terrain.

"I don't know," admitted the commander. "This slope is too slick and the crawler is overloaded." He paused, biting his lips as the vehicle skidded, treads chewing at the too-steep wall of rock before them. "I'll have to track, we'll never make it in a straight run."

"But the leeches?"

"We'll drop thermite at the end of every leg. It will have burned out by the time they get there, and the reduced heal output won't warn them away." His hand flickered to the thermal control and fire glowed in the darkness around them. "Come on, you black devils," he muttered. "Come and get a free meal."

The crawler lurched as he tugged at the steering levers, turning from the direct path to a criss-cross traversing of the slope, cutting down the actual gradient by extending the distance travelled. At the end of each journey as they turned and climbed painfully up the side of the mountain, crossing back and back again on the direct route, Lee flipped the switches and scattered burning thermite. The leeches, like trained dogs, obeyed their instinct and followed the path of the crawler, drawn by the radiated heat from the machine and the liberated energy of the compound.

Slowly the crawler drew ahead of the pursuers, and Lee sighed with relief as they drew level with the yawning mouth of the tunnel.

"Steady, Lee," warned Hughes. "Too much vibration and you'll bring the roof down."

"I know it." The young commander carefully nosed the vehicle over the lip of the hole. "We'll take it slow and use all searchlights. I think that we'll be safe as long as we don't touch the sides or vibrate too much." The speed of the crawler dropped to less than a slow walk as he adjusted the power lever, and the humming vibration from the spinning treads fell to a steady, almost gentle, drone.

Cautiously they crawled through the irregular, debris-littered tunnel, lights blazing and nerves tensed as they watched the slow retreat of the glittering ice and rock to either side.

Jack frowned.

"I don't get this," he said. "If you blasted your way through the roof should be strong enough to stand a little vibration. If it was that weak wouldn't it have collapsed before?"

"It might have," said Lacey grimly. "We were a long time coming through and for all we know the passage could be blocked, but that isn't the reason for us going slow now."

"No?"

"No. We used the thermite to make a passage, and that stuff contains plenty of heat. Some of it radiated up into the roof and it doesn't take much to melt frozen oxygen. This mountain is a mass of rock bound together by ice and snow. Once the snow has gone you get cavities, and the rock hangs together by spit and habit." He jerked a thumb upwards. "That's what we're afraid might have happened. Coming through the radiated heat didn't have much time to affect the rock, and we'd passed on before our vibration could do any damage. Now—"

He shrugged and, staring at the honeycomb pattern of the walls, Jack knew what he meant. He thinned his lips as he thought about it and was glad that Seth hadn't heard what the gaunt captain had said. An entire mountain of rock and ice rose above their heads, soaring miles high towards the stars—and the whole lot could come down at any moment.

It wasn't nice to think about.

They ate a few times, recklessly using the emergency thermocans to save power and time, and slept in shifts, each man driving until he felt that strain and fatigue was making him careless, then passing the controls to another operator. From time to time the commander tried the radio, but the mineral content of the rock reflected the wave, so that all they could hear was a droning hum.

"Maybe they've gone?" suggested Seth after Lacey had tried unsuccessfully to contact Weston. "Perhaps they think that you got crushed or something?"

"Weston won't desert," snapped Lee irritably. "I gave him strict orders."

"He might have gone at that," said Hughes thoughtfully.

"He knew how much air we carried and he couldn't guess that we found the ship and restocked. He might have waited until he knew we would normally have run out of air, and then given us up for dead and headed back to the Station."

Lacey turned white.

"That's right! And his own air wouldn't last for ever." He stared at Lee. "What shall we do if Weston's abandoned us?"

"Follow him."

"In this?" Lacey shook his head as he listened to the drone of the engine and the vibration of the treads. "We'd never make it. Some of the thermite must have melted part of the treads, I've noticed the jerking for a long while now. And anyway, what do we use for food?"

"We starve." Lee glared at the captain. "We don't even know that Weston's gone yet. What's the good of talking about it until we're sure?"

"Shut up," snapped Lee impatiently. He stared at the control panel. "If I'm right, and I think I am, then we'll know for sure in a little while. We are almost at the end of the tunnel." He grinned at Hughes who was driving. "Take it easy now, this part is probably weaker than the rest."

Hughes nodded, his eyes narrowed as he stared at the beam-lit walls of rock, and gently he began to case the crawler around a sharp bend.

"I remember this bit," said Lacey excitedly. "We made our first enfilade here, cut at an angle to shelter the crawler from the blast. I—" He broke off, his eyes wide with startled horror. "Look out!" His hand gripped Hughes by the shoulder. "The roof! It's caving in!"

Ahead, looking like jewels as they drifted slowly to the floor, glistening in the glare of the searchlights, a thin stream of dislodged rock and fragments of ice cascaded from above. Even as they watched the thin trickle increased, aggravated by the jarring vibration of the damaged treads, and larger pieces of stone fell from the sagging roof.

"Full speed!" ordered Lee, and his hand slapped down the power level. "Run for it, Hughes, and to hell with hitting the walls. Crash through."

The driver nodded, gripping the levers with white-knuckled hands, and with the skill of long experience sent the vehicle slewing as it jerked forward. It skidded, the treads ripping great quantities of rock from the collapsing walls, then straightened, lurching and swaying as it drove directly towards the falling curtain of rock.

Sound thundered through the cabin, the smashing impact of boulders as they fell on the curved hull of the crawler, and above the transmitted noise came the screaming whine of the engine as Hughes fed power to the spinning treads.

For a moment the vehicle shuddered, seeming to slow and yield to the crashing mass of rock falling from above them, as the sweating captain jerked at the controls, it slewed forward, scraped along a wall and lunged forward with a tearing grate from the damaged treads.

"Made it!" Lacey wiped sweat from his streaming features. "By space, we've made it!"

Hughes grunted as he juggled the controls, casing the strain on the ruined tread and slewing the vehicle in a series of shuddering lunges. Ahead of them, bright in the searchlight glare, a ragged opening gaped and light touched its edges, light from the crawlers below.

Engines whined as they reached the edge of the hole, shrilling as the heavy vehicle plunged down the slope, and behind them the mountain spurted shattered rock and powdered ice as the tunnel yielded to tremendous pressure and collapsed with soundless violence.

But ahead of them waited Weston and the two undamaged crawlers.

They were safe—and the beam control was safe with them.

CHAPTER 13

The room was quiet with a low susurration of sound, the eternal, never-ceasing hum of the Station, a sound which would be noise if it wasn't there.

Carl Dirac sighed as he put down the last tiny transistor of the dismantled beam control analytical banks, and wearily rubbed his tired eyes. It had been a long job this examination of the unit, a tedious, nerve-sapping task, with thousands of transistors and tubes, a complex pattern of wires and relays as complex almost as the human cortex.

But now it was over.

He looked up as the doctor entered the room and relaxed in his chair, the clutter of dismantled apparatus lying on the desk before him. The medico nodded towards it as he lit a cigarette.

"Any luck?"

"Yes—and no." Dirac stirred the glistening tubes with the tip of his quivering finger. "I know now why the unit failed, but I don't know how the failure was caused. The analytical banks show unmistakable signs of overloading, their normal operative current is very small as you know, and somehow a surge of electro-magnetic energy ruined the setting and built up a destructive feedback current in the circuits."

He stared at the doctor. "The question now is, how did this current enter the casing? It was insulated, away from any energy source other than that essential to maintain its operation, and that flow was safeguarded by triple fuses." He shook his head. "I must admit that the problem baffles me."

"That makes two of us, Carl." The doctor stared at the glowing tip of his cigarette. "You know of my own discoveries?"

"I have read the report, but really, what you claim is impossible."

"Is it?" Strangely enough the doctor didn't get annoyed. He pointed towards the litter of apparatus, and smoke plumed from between his lips. "As impossible as your own machine breaking down?"

"Machines always break down," said the old man defiantly. "The analogy, while interesting, has no real application to fact."

"And yet I state, and my assistants verified my findings, that the dead man showed unmistakable traces of motion after death." Abruptly the medico slammed his hand on to the desk. "Damn it, Carl! You believe what you see when it comes to machines. Why not give me credit for knowing my own profession?"

"Dead men do not walk," said the old man firmly. "To think otherwise is ridiculous."

"Are you afraid to admit the concept?" The doctor shrugged. "A man is dead, therefore that's the end of him; therefore nothing we can do to the body can be of any importance." He let twin streamers of smoke rill from his nostrils. "Do you think I haven't brooded about it? I'm a doctor, remember, and I've dissected more men than I like to think about. Always it seemed a harmless thing to do—the men were dead, weren't they? And the dead cannot feel. But then we never thought the dead could walk either, but they can, I've proved it, and if they can walk—"

"Don't torment yourself," said the old doctor gently. "The dead can't feel, you have done no wrong and caused no pain to helpless tissue."

"Thank you." The medico wiped sweat from his working features, and the hand that lifted the cigarette trembled as badly as his companion's. "But how can I be sure? How can I ever again be certain?"

"You will be certain—later. Now you are struggling to admit the impossible, and it is the impossible, you know. Hendris, no matter what you may have discovered, died out there on the day side, spilling his life with his air through his smashed helmet."

"I know that. I saw him." The doctor crushed out the butt of his cigarette. "He's the first man since the Station was built to die that way. With the front of his helmet smashed in. There have been other deaths, of course, but usually the suit has been intact when the bodies were recovered."

"So?" Dirac shrugged and rubbed at his red eyes. "This is getting us nowhere." He rose from the chair. "I'm going up into the Control Tower, perhaps Lee has returned within radio range by now."

"I'll join you," said the doctor, and together they walked to the elevator and up into the slender, thousand-foot-high tower.

From the instrument-cluttered room they stared at the familiar scene below.

"The sand devils are getting to be a nuisance." The medico pointed to where the pluming columns of the spinning energies whirled in ever-changing patterns. "See how they cluster around the vehicle shed." He shook his head and frowned. "You know, Carl, looking at those things I sometimes wonder if they couldn't be alive."

"Without bodies?" Carl frowned as he thought about it. "Surely if they were they would have tried to communicate with us by now? We've been here twenty years, remember, and not once in all that time have they made any attempt to contact us." He shrugged, a little annoyed with himself for taking the doctor's casual words seriously.

"Maybe they are." The doctor pointed to where a group of the spinning columns had suddenly coalesced into a distorted image of a crawler. "See? Pictures?"

"Nonsense. Merely accidental overlapping of the energy fields."

"Perhaps." The medico seemed determined to argue the supposition to a logical end. "I wonder if they have always done things like that. You were here in the early days, Carl. Can you remember if the sand devils were as thick and as versatile as they are now?"

"Of course they were. I—" Dirac frowned as dim memory stirred within the confines of his skull. "You know," he said slowly. "I don't believe they did."

"Could we check in any way?"

"Perhaps. I think that the Control Officer keeps some sort of a record as to how many sand devils are visible each hour." He smiled. "It gives him something to break the monotony, counting them, I mean, and I believe the men run a pool on who guesses the nearest number at certain hours." He looked at the uniformed officer. "Is that correct?"

"Pardon, sir?"

"I was telling the doctor about the observations on the sand devils you keep. You do keep them, I suppose?"

"Yes, sir. We count them on the grid."

"Have you the old records here?"

"Copies of them, sir. Do you want to see them?"

"Please."

Carl leafed through the bound report pages, and his eyes flickered as they scanned the neat rows of numbers giving the count of the peculiar formations. He frowned, riffled pages, frowned again and made another check.

"You were right, doctor," the old man said slowly. "From the first records the number of sand devils counted every hour has increased more than five hundred percent." He slammed the volume of reports shut and handed it back to the officer. "I should have noticed it. Someone should have commented on it."

"Why should they?" The doctor shrugged as he fumbled for his inevitable cigarette. "It's not a thing a man would notice if it happened gradually over a long period of time. And who cares about them anyway? Why should anyone make it his business to worry about them?" He puffed the cigarette into life. "After all, they're harmless, an amusing diversion if you care for that sort of thing, as harmless as watching Terrestrial clouds."

"You think so?"

"I'm certain of it."

Carl nodded, staring with thoughtful eyes at the dancing shapes far below. He turned, narrowing his eyes as he stared towards the night side, then stared at the sand devils again.

"You know, doctor," he said slowly. "You've just given me the most incredible idea."

"I have?" Smoke writhed against the dimmed windows. "What?"

"You said the sand devils could be alive."

"Did I?" The doctor grinned. "Forget it. You should know by now that I'll argue on anything just as long as I'm on the opposite side."

"So? Then let us argue some more. What is life, doctor?"

"The ability to grow, remember and multiply." The medico shrugged. "That is one definition. Unfortunately there are certain metallic crystals that fill all those requirements. They grow in a solution, can multiply by cleavage—all crystals can do that—and they can remember. At least they are affected by a magnetic field, respond and, when again subject within a short space of time to similar energies, 'remember' and stay unaffected. There are chemicals which will do that also, their molecules respond to sunlight, and will respond the same way to artificial light, but not unless exposed to it within a short while of the natural light. Otherwise they sense the difference." He shrugged. "Trying to define life is a difficult business, Carl."

"And yet surely there are some definitions which must be fulfilled before a thing can be called 'alive'?"

"Yes, but understand that these are essentials of life, not that anything fulfilling them is alive." The doctor chuckled. A delicate point, perhaps, but essential when you come to think about it."

"I understand," said Carl quietly. "To say 'God is I', is not the same as saying 'I am God'."

"Exactly, just as it is incorrect to assume that a woman with child is the same thing as a woman and child." The doctor shrugged. "To get to the basics. Life must have the ability to grow, to multiply—breed if you like—and to be able to survive. It must have some form of energy, either the chemical oxidization cycle on which we live or, like the symbiotic parasites of Venus, be able to live on the energy of its host. Mobility isn't important, an oyster isn't mobile and neither is intelligence. Usually life cannot live among its own waste products, but we may yet find a form of life which doesn't have any, so that doesn't count."

"What do you mean by that?"

"Well, you and I and all known creatures, with the exception perhaps of the Venusian parasites, eat food in order to live. That food's basically a source of energy. But our metabolism isn't efficient enough to utilize it all and so there is a certain amount of waste. As that waste is useless to us we can't live on it, and as it is usually toxic it acts as a poison." He shrugged. "The first lesson in primary biology."

"How about plants? They're alive, aren't they?"

"Yes, but vegetation by-passed some of our food problems eons ago. A plant extracts its food from the soil and air, the sunlight and water. Photo-synthesis they call it, and plants take their energy direct instead of having to have it processed for them as we do." He chuckled. "It's like us drinking milk. The milk really comes from the grass the cow eats, but we can't eat grass, and so we have to wait until the cow can process it into something edible."

"Then theoretically it should be possible for us to live on a direct source of energy?"

"Not without metabolism. A robot can do it because it's designed to use straight electricity for power, and a robot has no waste products aside from the discharged accumulators."

"But theoretically it would be possible?"

"Yes," said the doctor slowly. "I suppose it would. An alien life form consisting of pure energy should—" He paused, his eyes narrowing as he stared at the writhing shapes of the sand devils. "Carl! You—"

"Yes," said the old man quietly, then before the other could speak he hurried on. "Why not? You said that an entity could live on pure energy, and where else can more energy be found than on a planet very close to a sun? Mercury is such a place, drenched continuously by the searing heat and radiation of our own star. A pattern of balanced forces, a web of electro-magnetic energy, a field of force if you wish, and—?"

"I don't like what you're saying," said the doctor thickly. "I don't like it at all."

"But it's possible?"

"Perhaps."

"As possible as a dead man walking?" Carl stared sombrely at the white-faced medico. "It would explain a lot, you know."

"It would explain everything," admitted the doctor. "But really, Carl. Do you know what you're saying?"

"Yes."

"You're standing there and telling me that—"

"I'm telling you that the sand devils are alive! That for twenty years now we've stared at them, being amused and annoyed by them, and never in all that time did we even imagine that we were staring at native Mercutians!

Silence fell as the two men stared at the writhing columns, and as if in silent mockery the spinning shapes joined, coalesced and reformed in a vast, grinning face. The face of a dead man.

Hendris!

CHAPTER 14

For a moment it stayed there, a face of dust on the grey plain, a grimacing, somehow faintly obscene visage, then, as the patterns always did, it crumpled and fell, spreading its content over the rolling plain.

"The answer," whispered Carl sickly. "A man lying dead out on the plain, a man with a smashed face plate and nothing between his flesh and the sand devils. Perhaps they entered into him, engaging their web of force with the nervous system, and then, who knows?"

"I knew that the corpse had moved," said the doctor, and the sound of his right fist slamming into his left palm echoed through the humming silence of the observation room. "Dennison must have seen him, and to a man in his state such a shock would prove fatal."

"Why did they do it?" Carl sighed as he stared out at the heat-seared plain. "Curiosity perhaps?" He shrugged. "It doesn't matter, the facts remain. An alien life form entered the dead man's body, was carried into the Station and there, in the quiet and silence, made the dead man walk."

"But could it have done?" A frown marred the doctor's forehead. "We know that they can scoop up a little dust, but there is a big difference between a handful of powdered rock and the mass of a full-grown man. Wouldn't the weight have defeated them?"

"It didn't, did it?" Carl stared down at his trembling hands. "In a way it would be so much easier, for a man isn't a pile of inert matter as the dust is, a man has a complex nervous system and we know that muscular reaction is electrical in nature. All the entity would have to do would be to mesh with that nervous system, use its own energy to operate the synapses, and the muscles would bunch and move. A frog's leg will do the same thing beneath an electrical flow; didn't Benjamin Franklin stumble on that fact ages ago?"

"Yes."

"They must have had trouble at first, perhaps stumbled into the hospital ward and shocked Dennison to his death. Then they found the beam Control, a far more useful vehicle for their type of energy, and the entity left the dead man, entered the analytical banks—and ruined them by too high a current flow."

"Perhaps they meant to do that all the time?"

"Perhaps." Carl sighed as he stared at the grotesque shapes writhing below. "Or perhaps they were just curious. All this shaping of the dust, the ever-changing combinations, of semi-familiar objects, is it due to a desire to communicate or—"

"Attack?" The doctor stared at the old man. "Is it possible?"

"They ruined the beam control," reminded Carl. "And yet I can't believe that they are really inimical. Why should they be? We don't threaten them in any way, their source of energy, their food, is beyond our reach, and they have nothing which we want or could use. Neither do we own anything they want." He shook his head as he stared out across the plain. "Just one more mystery of the hell planet."

"It may not be such a mystery as you think," said the doctor slowly. "Don't let us make the mistake of crediting them with too high an intelligence." He smiled at the old man's puzzled expression. "Assuming that they are alive, aware and conscious, able to direct their movements and energies. I think we must assume that there is no other explanation as to what has happened. Well, then, don't their actions remind you of something?"

"No," said the old man thoughtfully. "I don't think so." He blinked. "Children?"

"Perhaps, but I see them as primitives. They have lived here for who can guess how long? Living on a barren, monotonous plain, living their restricted lives without break or change. And then we came. Something new, exciting, interesting. We brought gifts with us, and for the sand devils life became full of interest."

"Gifts?"

"Of course." The doctor pointed to where a spinning column writhed in continuous flux. "The human brain is essentially an electrical instrument, thought an electrical process. What more natural than that the sand devils should be able to pick up the intangible broadcasts from our brains? Dimly, of course, for no man has ever gone unshielded on to the plains, but the pictures would be there, must be there, for how else would the sand devils be able to copy things known only to men?"

"Telepathic!" Carl sucked in a deep breath and his eyes glistened. "If we could contact them—" He shrugged. "But how? And we have other things to worry about now. Lee is overdue and the ships are heading in from Earth. Unless he returns with the beam control they will crash." He swallowed as he thought about it, and turned to the silent Control Officer. "Any word from the search party?"

"None, sir."

"I see." The old man nodded and stared towards the mysterious regions of the night side. Nothing. Just the eternal rolling waste of the libration area, the black sky glowing with the points of many stars, and the long, thin shadow of the tower pointing like a gigantic finger towards the regions of utter frigidity. Carl stood for a moment, staring up at the burning points of the distant suns, and he smiled a little as he found the tiny, greenish-white star that was Earth.

Home.

A home he had never seen for the past twenty years. A place of sweet memory, of dimly remembered seas, of snow and glittering ice. A world of rolling grass and bare, brown mountains, of blue skies and fleecy clouds. A world of beauty and fair promise, of wistful longing and heart-tearing dreams. Home.

The doctor gripped his arm and pointed with one finger.

"Look."

"What is it?" Carl frowned, a little annoyed at being interrupted from his nostalgic dreaming, then thinned his lips as he saw what the medico pointed at.

A pluming column of writhing dust hurled itself towards the Control Tower.

There was no bulk to it, of course, the entire thing consisted of no more than a few pounds of sand, but as it struck the instrument dials flickered in wild confusion and a peculiar tingling jarred through the bodies of the watching men.

"What the hell was that?" The officer stared at them, his face pale and his eyes wide with shock. "I've never seen anything like it before."

"What damage?" Carl stepped towards the instruments, and his old eyes flickered over the dials. The officer shrugged.

"Not much, this place was built to withstand radiation, but I'll bet that some of the radio tubes have been ruined."

"Electro-magnetic energy," said the old man.

"Yes." He nodded. "Repair the radio if necessary. I'm going below."

Together he and the doctor rode the humming elevator down to the huddled buildings below.

"Primitives, you said." Carl rubbed his chin. "Tell me, what are the attributes to be expected if your theory is right?"

"Lack of responsibility. Erratic behaviour. A simple delight in trifles and a desire for company. Most primitives are quite uncomplicated. They like to play, amuse themselves, and at the same time have no concept of anything more important than their own pleasure."

"Vindictive?"

"No, not normally at least, but like a child they will at times deliberately annoy in order to attract attention." He glanced at the old man. "You've got an idea?"

"Yes." Carl led the way from the elevator and into his bedroom. "You said that the sand devils were primitive. Would you say that their behaviour fits that definition?"

"It could. Curiosity, amusement at emulating the dim thought images radiated from the armoured men, and discovery that it was possible to enter the dead body. Curiosity would have driven them to make that experiment, and once within the Station the same motive would make them explore." The doctor shrugged. "With, I assume, fatal results. Am I correct?"

"It was possible that the electro-magnetic energy of the alien was disrupted by the analytical banks," said Carl. "More than possible. Metal would serve to ground the pattern, and even if they could pass that barrier, and the evidence is against it, the beam control energy flow would have heterodyned, cancelled out the invading energy." He stared at the doctor. "What are you getting at?"

"The primitives' love of attention. That is probably the main reason for their assuming the fantastic shapes that they do. Once a man's mind is concentrated on them they are probably able to pick up more images from his mind—more shapes, more attention. The impact on the tower was probably for the same reason."

"So I thought." Carl shook his head. "Fantastic! At any other time I would welcome the opportunity to investigate, but now we have more serious things to worry about."

"Lee?"

"Yes, and the beam control. Now is the worst possible time for the sand devils to disrupt radio service. That attack was a minor thing, but if more of them coalesced and made frequent attempts, we would be unable to use the beam control, radio, any external thing depending on electricity and a steady current flow." He bit his lip. "Something must be done about it."

"You have an idea?"

"Yes. If we can broadcast a pattern of energy waves, not of such a wavelength that they would disturb normal radio or the beam control, but able to irritate the sand devils so that they would retreat from the Station and leave us in peace—" He nodded. "Will you help me? My hands—" He held out his quivering fingers, and the doctor nodded.

"Of course."

It took ten days. Ten days during which the sand devils spun in ever increasing numbers around the domes of the station, filling the Twilight Belt with their spinning grotesque shapes. Radio service had degenerated into a slurred hum of static, with tubes burning out as the surging tides of alien energy built up destroying feed-back circuits, and Carl knew that even if the beam control analytical banks were working, their signals would be distorted beyond all use by the free energies emitted from the aliens.

He hoped that his invention would solve that problem. It was a simple thing, a small Dirac accumulator mounted with a convoluted antenna of silver wire, coupled to an interrupter circuit and the whole thing firmly attached to the connections of the powerful battery.

"This won't harm them," he explained. "But what it should do is to broadcast a continually changing pattern of energy which will irritate the delicate balance of their energy fields." He smiled. "Much as water will not hurt a cat, but will annoy it so that it runs away."

"Shall we spread them around the Station?" The doctor gulped smoke and stared at the little thing he had helped to build. "We'd better hurry, Carl. The last message we had from the ships warned us that they were getting within deceleration range. Even without the beam control we need direct contact so as to talk them down. It won't help much, without that contact they won't stand a chance."

"I know it," said the old man tiredly. "Let's go and test this unit."

Outside, the plain was a mass of twisting shapes writhing in wild confusion, the spinning columns dashing sand against the armoured figures as they strode a few paces from the base of the slender tower. Carl staggered as a grinning skull drove at him, instinctively tried to dodge a charging monstrosity, and imagined that he heard the thin cackle of alien mirth as sand coated his glare-shields. The doctor's voice, thin, slurred, scarcely recognisable even over the distance of a few yards, echoed in the great helmet.

"Shall we try here, Carl?"

"Yes."

"Look at them," said the doctor as he set down the adapted accumulator. "Like a gang of kids out on a picnic." He grunted as whirling shapes resolved into the likeness of a crawler; then into a thing resembling a horse, then into a grey, cold metallic copy of a Dirac accumulator. "Just wait, you devils," he muttered. "I'll teach you a lesson."

He closed the circuit in the little machine.

At first nothing seemed to happen, the swirling columns raced towards them, spinning, dissolving, changing into more and more fantastic configurations, and in the helmets static hummed and blurred from the inter-suit radios. Then—

Carl was reminded of a gang of tom cats yowling on a fence, a bristle-tailed, hot-eyed bunch of animals yelling defiance to the lambent Moon. Then, as water sprayed on them, they had exploded into a mass of running, furry bodies.

So it was with the sand devils.

One second they were pressing all around the two men and, the oddly sparking machine, the next they had gone, the dust they had energised to form the tenuous images falling in a grey cloud, and suddenly the inter-suit radios hummed clear and free of all static other than the normal blur cast from the swollen sun.

The doctor chuckled.

"That taught them. Are you sure it didn't kill them, Carl?"

"Positive. See?" The old man pointed with his armoured hand, squinting through his glare-shields as he stared towards the searing horizon of the day side. From the radio he heard the doctor chuckle again as he saw the twisting line of distant shapes rising and coalescing as they vented their annoyance in images formed from the powdered dust.

Someone had been intensely angry at one dome and the aliens had picked up the thought images from his mind. Now they were using them, and Carl felt his face grow hot at what he saw.

"The devils!" He swallowed as he heard the doctor laugh. "I'll—"

"Take it easy, Carl." The doctor pulled at his arm. "We've got to make more of these little contraptions to keep the area free of interference. Anyway, I'm glad that the things aren't really hurt, I'd miss them now, and in a way they're quite amusing."

A fresh voice broke in, echoing strongly from the radios.

"Message from the Control Tower. The search party has been sighted."

"Can you see them?"

"No, sir. The message was relayed from one of the crawlers, the one the Commander left at the edge of the Twilight Belt.

"Did they find the ship?"

"I don't know, sir. The crawler had to break radio contact with them before it could contact us."

"I see." Carl stared through the glare-shields, his pale, washed-out blue eyes thoughtful. "I'll be right up."

Together he and the doctor entered the base of the tower, removing their armour as they passed through the airlock, and remaining silent as they rode up the elevator. The Control Officer turned as they entered the room.

"I've just made full contact, sir. The crawler at the edge of the Twilight Belt is acting as a relay. Do you wish—"

Carl almost snatched the microphone.

"Lee?"

"Hello, Carl."

"Did you find them, Lee? The ship, the component, your brother and the rest?"

"We found them." A great weariness seemed to weigh the young commander's voice. "My brother is safe, Carl, and so is the beam control. We lost one crawler, abandoned it near the wreck, one day perhaps we'll go back for it. Blain's got a broken leg; have the hospital warned and in readiness, will you?"

"I'll do that." Carl hesitated, staring through the dimmed windows towards the glare-lit horizon. The sand devils were there. "How long will you be, Lee? Need any help?"

"We won't be long and we can manage." The Commander chuckled. "Wait until I get back, Carl. I've something to tell you, an alien life form we found on the night side, it's incredible!"

"Is it?" Carl swallowed as he stared at the posturing swirling dust on the horizon. "Maybe I've a surprise for you, too."

He set down, the microphone as the Commander chuckled and stared sombrely towards the spinning columns of the distant sand devils.

He had been twenty years on the hell planet and had only once ever really lost his temper. It seemed as if he wasn't going to be allowed to forget it.

On the horizon electro-magnetic forces picked up a heap of grey dust, energised it, moulded it to an invisible pattern and—

A ten times life-sized figure of an unmistakable old man thumbed his nose at the slender tower of the Station.

Somehow Carl knew that he would never be able to live it down.